TRADERS IN ARMS

A James Gunn Novel

Robbie J Robertson

Three Wolves Publishing

Copyright © 2024 Robert James Robertson

All rights reserved

The characters and events portrayed in this book are fictitious. Any similarity to real persons, living or dead, is coincidental and not intended by the author.

No part of this book may be reproduced, or stored in a retrieval system, or transmitted in any form or by any means, electronic, mechanical, photocopying, recording, or otherwise, without express written permission of the publisher.

ISBN-13: 9798868133503
ISBN-10: 1477123456

Cover design by: Art Painter
Library of Congress Control Number: 2018675309
Printed in the United States of America

For my father

Bob Robertson, 1923-2017

A great country can have no such thing as a little war.

DUKE OF WELLINGTON

CONTENTS

Title Page
Copyright
Dedication
Epigraph

Chapter One. The Double	1
Chapter Two. The Insider	21
Chapter Three. Success	36
Chapter Four. The Gathering Storm	50
Chapter Five. Taking the Bait	73
Chapter Six. Invasion	79
Chapter Seven. The Incident	97
Chapter Eight. The Rendezvous	110
Chapter Nine. My Brilliant Friend	123
Chapter Ten. The Spy Who Came in from the Cold	157
Chapter Eleven. The Plan	174
Chapter Twelve. Victory	189
Chapter Thirteen. Revelations	208

Chapter Fourteen. Secrets	220
Afterword	227
Acknowledgement	231
About The Author	233
Books By This Author	235

CHAPTER ONE.
THE DOUBLE

The rain swept across La Place de La Bourse, as James Gunn made his way up the steps of the exchange and out of the foul January weather. It had been raining for days, and the great columns of the Palais Brongniart were washed as dark grey as the leaden skies above. The swarm of umbrella-wielding *agents de change* jostled through the grand entrance in their haste to escape the glowering Paris skies.

He pushed his way through the arches of the dealing floor to the little office of Leclerc Proust, and throwing open the glass-panelled door, tossed his dripping overcoat onto the laden coat stand.

Gunn had joined Leclerc's small Paris team in December 1981 and in a few short weeks had built a reputation as an ambitious trader on the exchange floor. As a Scot, he stood out from the handful of English brokers, and his university background made him something of an enigma within the trading community. And he had brought something novel to Leclerc's Paris office: he produced research. As well as executing the dealing instructions which came daily from

London, he had begun to put together some basic advice for the firm's partners to pass on to their clients.

He had been hired the previous autumn by Beloe and Stringer, the senior and managing partners of Leclerc, to begin to rejuvenate the fortunes of the venerable, but ailing firm. The pressure for change was building in the City of London, and through graduates like James and his peers the partners saw the opportunity to get ahead of the competition.

'Ah, c'est l'Écossais. Good morning Jamie, m'Lord'. The wiry figure of Pierre Gavanche greeted him with his usual enthusiasm from behind the mountain of reports which were piled high on his creaking desk.

'Morning Pierre. It's bloody foul out there. The Métro was awash, and the streets are running like rivers. Anything new from London?'

Gavanche turned to answer, in his distinctive mixture of English and French.

'Toujours le same thing. Les Brits - ils pensant que nous sommes toxiques et Mitterrand est le diable.'

Pierre was the office manager of Leclerc-Paris. A sharp-witted and restless character, the Bourse was in Pierre's blood. He was the fourth generation of his family to tread the worn boards of the dealing floor. For Pierre, life on the Bourse had long ago ceased to be about the accumulation of wealth, for he had more money than he could ever imagine how to spend. Yet he took no holidays, spent very little on clothes or indulgences for himself, and spent every hour possible in the exchange building or the numerous bars and restaurants in the surrounding streets. It was through Pierre's family ties with one of the official *agents de change*, that Leclerc was able to trade using its own name.

James began to prepare his dealing books as he responded.

'Well - I guess that's understandable. You can't blame our clients in London for wanting absolutely nothing to do with this infernal socialist State. Think about the beating they took last May when Mitterrand won the election - the market collapsed. It was a disaster'.

James gathered his things and straightened his tie.

'But despite the gloom, we've got to keep our chins up, my old mate, and remember, nothing goes in straight lines. Something will turn up. Which reminds me - I have to finish my report on the nationalisation plan. Did Steve call from London about our meeting tomorrow?'

'Oui bien sûr. He can see you at ten for coffee, m'Lord. Traders. Rue de la Bourse.'

'Excellent. I'm looking forward to picking his not inconsiderable brain.'

'Je ne comprends pas. You are very amusing Monsiour l'Écossais!'

'Well, thank you Pierre. Most kind. But could you

please stop calling me 'm'Lord'. Your English is a cross between the Financial Times and a Mills and Boon novel.'

James strode towards the door to the dealing floor, and turning with a flourish, exclaimed;

'But now you must *excuse moi* as I venture forth once more into the Temple of Mammon, and work my way through today's miserable orders! All sells I suppose. Oh - and Pierre - see you later at Le Vaudeville?'

'Absolument, m'Lord. A bientôt,' Pierre called back to James's retreating figure.

He took up his position on the equity market floor, and nodded curt greetings to the other traders. The high vaulted and galleried interior rose up to the giant skylight, through which James could see the rain continuing to fall and spread into shapes across the roof, like grey lava moving across a glass landscape. Then the auction began, just as it had done on this same spot for over one hundred and fifty years.

James held back at first. He had only a handful of buy orders but a large fistful of sells, and the other traders could easily guess what his clients wanted to do. They were very happy to offer him stock - they knew he was unlikely to accept their generous terms. But they offered only the poorest of prices for the stocks which they guessed he'd been instructed to sell. Each day was the same.

He could buy any amount of stock he wished, but selling was becoming increasingly difficult. The pack of brokers now retreating from the auction to their offices around the Bourse were confident that Leclerc's clients were unlikely to reinvest in a France which had seen markets rattled and its currency devalued under the Mitterrand regime.

James gathered his coat, and stood for a moment on the steps of the market, looking across the square to the restaurant beyond. As he watched the rain bouncing off the flagstones, he reflected on the way his life had changed over the few months since he'd come down from Oxford. A series of events in London had conspired to hasten his posting to Paris after the minimum of training in the City. And he had quickly embraced his new role and the new excitements that Paris offered. It was all a very long way from where he had started, in the grey, graffiti-scarred monotony of his home town in Scotland.

He had felt pretty relaxed about leaving London behind, although he did have some misgivings over the rushed manner of his departure. There was a girl he'd grown close to. He felt something very different about her in a way that he hadn't really felt about any other girl before. He wished now that he'd shared his feelings with Lucinda before he'd left. But he hadn't. And then Polly had arrived. And Polly had changed everything.

His old college friend David, had called him in December to say that he'd bumped into Polly Peters at a dinner party in the history faculty.

'She was asking after you, Jamie. Said she'd love to see you again in Paris. Turns out that she's spending six months in your neck of the woods. A couple of terms at the Sorbonne. Hope you don't mind, but I gave her the number of your office over there.'

'No problem at all, Dave. The Sorbonne's literally a stone's throw from my flat at the Panthéon. Tell her to call me and I'll buy her dinner.'

James was intrigued. He and Polly had spent a night together the previous summer after a drunken party to celebrate his graduation. She was very beautiful, very confident, and James had been swept along by her charm and charisma. So when she called his office, he had arranged for them to meet at the romantic Polidor restaurant. And James couldn't pretend to himself that he wasn't without some hope that the evening might turn out to be just as intimate as his choice of setting.

He had dressed carefully for dinner; the double-breasted pinstripe suit which had become his new work uniform, brightened up by a rich Hermès tie. He arrived early, chose a discreet table by the window, and ordered a bottle of Lanson. The other diners spoke in hushed tones and were also formally dressed - suits for the men, and an assortment of elegant outfits for the women. So when Polly swept into the restaurant all heads turned as she threw her arms around James and kissed him enthusiastically, her bright red lipstick leaving a perfectly-formed pair of lips on his cheek. She was dressed in Doc Martens, tight black leather trousers, and a loose-fitting BOY tee shirt, its distinctive eagle logo spread across her chest. Her hair was arranged in a 'new romantic' style, which for a moment made him think of Duran Duran.

'Jamie, it's amazing to see you again! It's really nice of you to take me out - and what a fantastic place! This is a world away from the student union cafe. Wow! You've ordered champagne. Can we have some?'

'Sure - of course. It's fantastic to see you too Polly.' James motioned for the waiter to pour a couple of glasses. 'So, you're here for a few months. How did that come about?'

'Well. This really brilliant opportunity came up, and I just had to grab it. The Oxford history faculty decided to arrange an exchange with half a dozen colleges around Europe, and I jumped at the chance to see a bit of the world. I've always loved Paris, so I elected to come here, and it all worked out perfectly!'

'I see. Sounds great! And where are you living? Are you in student halls?'

Polly lifted the champagne flute to her lips and downed its contents in one. Her tee shirt had slid off her right shoulder, causing their fellow female diners to react with some consternation, as they muttered to their partners to stop staring and concentrate on their menus.

'Yes. And they're absolute crap!' Polly's voice rose, causing more scowls and sharp intakes of breath. 'We're four to a dorm, the heating is rubbish and last night we saw a fucking mouse! Otherwise it's fine.' She laughed, and James found himself caught up in her unselfconscious good humour.

'So what about you, Jamie. Where are your digs?'

'Actually I've been very fortunate. My Paris colleague owns several flats which he rents out and he's letting me stay in one at a knock-down price. It's on the top floor of a rather attractive building just beside the Panthéon. I have a little terrace which looks out over the great dome, and all the way north to le Sacré-Cœur.'

'Wow! Sounds crazy! I'd love to see it some time. You seem to be doing really well Jamie.' Polly's voice rose as she became even more enthused. 'I know we only met briefly in Oxford, and I know that we spent most of the evening screwing, but I did form a really lovely impression of you.'

She leant forward, a broad smile on her lips, and she lowered her voice, 'It was quite a memorable night wasn't it, Jamie?'

The restaurant was now silent, as the diners strained to hear their conversation. James couldn't suppress an embarrassed smile.

'Well. Yes. I mean - you're quite something, Polly.

You're quite a force of nature. Look, let's enjoy the food here - it's great by the way - and then we can go for a few drinks around the Luxembourg Gardens and I can show you my flat, if you're still interested that is.'

'I am interested, Jamie. In fact I'm very interested indeed!' Polly replied deliberately, before downing another glass of the fast-disappearing champagne.

James ordered a bottle of Sancerre, and they laughed as Polly grappled with the frogs legs which she eventually ate with much theatrical grimacing. Then a bottle of Burgundy followed along with the steaks, and finally a couple of brandies while they decided which route to take to the Pantheon. They walked arm in arm down Rue Corneille towards the Luxembourg Gardens and when they reached Café le Rostand, they took a seat facing the grand garden buildings.

'Do you fancy a nightcap, Polly, or do you think we've had enough?'

She leant across the little drinks table, and pulled him towards her. They kissed for what seemed like an eternity, and as he sat back, she motioned to the waiter and replied.

'No Jamie. I think we're just beginning. Let's drink a toast to picking up from where we left off!'

James smiled to himself as he recalled the end of that evening, Polly's shrieks of delight when she saw his flat, and the scene of chaos the next morning, when they eventually awoke to a tangled jumble of sheets, pillows and clothes. And then she had turned up that afternoon with her suitcase, rucksack and briefcase, and she hadn't left. He still felt a little vague about how exactly it had all come about so quickly, but now she was a permanent fixture in his life. They were a couple. He lived with Polly.

A group of brokers pushing their way past jolted James out of his reverie and back down to earth. And back to the gloomy predictability of Leclerc's current business. If things continued like this, the firm was going to struggle. He turned his raincoat collar up against the downpour and dashed across the rain-drenched square for an early lunch at Le Vaudeville. And as he ran, he began to form the outline of a plan which, if successful, might see him turn his competitors' confidence and complacency to his and to Leclerc's advantage. But it all depended on his making some real progress with the report on Mitterrand's nationalisation plans which Beloe had asked him to write. James had an instinct that the market was underestimating the amount of compensation which the government would eventually have to pay to shareholders in the several companies and banks which were to be taken into State ownership. At the moment the sum being suggested stood at almost $6 billion, but he had a hunch that it would end up being much higher.

James hung up his raincoat, shook some rain out of his hair, and made his way through the clatter and hubbub of the grand old restaurant. The brokers and bankers were already filling the long banquettes, talking loudly to be heard above the din. Waiters in long white aprons were weaving their way expertly between the tables, carrying platters of seafood and trays laden with drinks. The beer and wine were already flowing freely, despite the early hour. It felt like a typical Monday. Weekend hangovers were being gently soothed by the first few glasses of the week.

James walked past the tables and asked an elegantly dressed gentleman sitting at the bar if the neighbouring bar stools were free. Placing his copy of the FT carefully on the polished oak surface between himself and the stranger, he exchanged a few pleasantries, and waited for Pierre to arrive.

James ordered '*un demi*' and as he was savouring the refreshing taste of the draft beer, Pierre arrived and took up position on the bar stool next to him. His neatly cut hair was soaked from his quick sprint across the square, and a couple of droplets fell onto the bar as he ordered a beer.

'It looks like you swam here, Pierre. I thought this kind of weather was confined to damp old Britain!'

'Oui. Ce temps est de la merde. What is looking

tasty today m'Lord?'

'I think I'll just have a few oysters, and a glass of champagne. Don't want to muddle the brain too much. Got to make the grey matter work this afternoon.'

'Matière gris?'

'Doesn't matter - about the matter. Look, I'm at the final stages of putting my case together on the nationalisation stocks and I'd like to know what you think. Mitterrand has said he'll take five industrial groups, two investment houses, and countless banks into State ownership. The question is how much he will eventually pay for them?'

'C'est difficile. Where are the examples of successful companies being nationalised?'

'That's the problem. There are very few exact precedents. I've looked at all the UK nationalisations since the war, but they're of limited relevance. They're just not that helpful. I've ended up trying to read between the lines of the Senate's comments and the rhetoric coming out of the foreign shareholders.'

Pierre took a long sip of beer and thought for a moment.

'Jamie. The constitution says the process has to be rapide et équitable, prompt and fair as you say. What do you think that means?'

'I don't know. What does 'fair' mean for shareholders in St.-Gobain, Rhône-Poulenc and the other companies? If you value their shares using their weak prices since the election, you're looking at a fairly low figure. It's just that I can't help feeling that the foreign shareholders are going to dig their heels in and extract their pound of flesh.'

James studied Pierre's look of blank incomprehension, and exhaled loudly.

'Let's just get the grub in, shall we Pierre? And let's make it a bottle of champagne. Let's hope it oils the mental wheels!'

The typical working day for an average *agent de change* was less than arduous; a late start, followed by a short shares auction, and then a long lunch, which left just enough time for a brief visit to the office before early evening drinks. And today was proving to be no exception. The oysters were followed by plates of charcuterie, and then succulent chicken in a wine sauce, and finally creme brûlée. Pierre insisted on ordering a bottle of Beaujolais to wash down the meal. He had been celebrating the arrival of the new vintage now for several weeks. Pierre regarded it as a light wine - just slightly more alcoholic than water, and perfect for lunchtime drinking.

A couple of hours later, and feeling quite reinvigorated, James stood up to settle the bill. The gentleman to his left had just departed, and had left his copy of Le Figaro next to James's FT. He picked up both papers and slid them into his raincoat pocket before he and Pierre hurried across the square and back to the Leclerc Proust office.

Pierre called London to record the day's bargains - the list of purchases and sales which they'd made - and to give a short market report. James settled behind his antique pedestal desk and stared blankly at the electric typewriter. He inserted a fresh sheet of A4. So far his report had lots of historic references, but little which would convince investors of a case for buying the nationalisation stocks. All it had was his instinct that they presented an opportunity. He needed some insight into the way their international shareholders were thinking, and how far they would push the government. His meeting tomorrow with Steve was his last hope of producing something interesting. An old fellow-lodger from his time in London, Steve was now moving up through the ranks of Her Majesty's Treasury at an astounding rate. He was visiting some large private investors in Paris on a project which he'd been unable to discuss on the phone, and James hoped that he'd be able to provide some of the ideas which he badly needed.

He stared out at the grey skies, and thought about tomorrow's conference call with London. He would be presenting to the senior management group: Marcus Stringer, managing partner and violent sceptic, who thought that any investment in France was a sure sign of imbecility, and Douglas Elgin, head of strategy and a fellow Scot. Douglas was a giant of a man, both in stature and in terms of his big-hearted support for James and the other graduates. Then there was Miriam Goldberg, head of research and an intimidating mixture of intellect and street-wise instinct. And finally there would be Percival Beloe, senior partner. Behind the self-effacing modesty there was a calculating and decisive mind. He had the final word, and took full responsibility for the key decisions. The others respected all the nerve which that took.

Pierre finished his calls and gathered his things to head back to the Vaudeville.

'Peut-être a beer, Jamie? One for the road, as you say.'

'Actually, I have to dash. I'm meeting Polly at Le Café de la Paix in twenty minutes. We've got tickets to the Police concert this evening out at Le Bourget. I'm off to the loo to change, so see you tomorrow.'

James quickly changed into Levis and a parka, and put the newspapers and his suit into a rucksack, before heading along to l'Opéra. He and Polly loved The Police, and she thought that Sting was the most gorgeous man in the world. He was looking forward to forgetting about work for a few hours.

James hurried along Rue du 4 Septembre, and then turned into le Place de l'Opéra. He paused to marvel afresh at the splendour of the opera house, the eight pairs of giant columns reaching up into the murky evening sky, the gilded figures of Harmony and Poetry still shining brightly despite the swirling rain. As he gazed upwards a voice rose above the din of the traffic, and looking across the square, he could see Polly gesticulating wildly towards him. She had managed to find a table tucked under the long canopy which ran the length of the cafe, and now she was waving a bottle of wine in enthusiastic greeting.

James squeezed on to the wicker chair next to her, and wrapped his arms around her. Polly was wearing a fake fur coat which she had picked up in a secondhand shop in Les Halles. The rain had turned it a sleek brown - more rabbit than mink - but Polly had a way of looking stunning whatever she wore.

'How's the report coming along?' she asked, 'Did you meet Steve? Did you have any other interesting meetings?'

James liked the way she took an interest in his work, although he preferred to hear about her day.

'No, I'm meeting him tomorrow. And it was a fairly quiet day. Had a light lunch with Pierre, and otherwise - pretty uneventful. How about you?'

Polly proceeded to give an account of her day, which involved much exaggerated mimicking of tutors and much elaborate waving around of her wine glass. She made James laugh, and as they tucked into their omelettes and frites he thought about how happy this part of his life was - the Bourse, his colleagues, and this very definition of effervescence sitting before him. Each of these things were placed in their own separate drawers in his mind, and only he could see the entire contents.

He would never be able to share them all with Polly.

The Ghost in the Machine performance was fantastic and by the time the band had performed a second encore, James and Polly had become part of a sweating, writhing crowd which eventually stumbled out of the Rotonde and into the rail system.

Back in the flat at the Panthéon, James fixed a negroni and took it onto the terrace, where he sat under the canvas and gazed through the mist and rain towards the lights of Sácre-Cœur. Six floors below, on the cobbled forecourt of the Panthéon, the last stragglers from the bars and restaurants moved quickly through the streets, raincoats buttoned to the neck, and brollies, briefcases and newspapers held aloft against the pitiless downpour. He opened his rucksack and drew out his report and the newspapers. Checking that Polly was still in the shower, he opened Le Figaro and began to study its contents. After twenty minutes or so, he stepped back into the study, and walked quietly to the bedroom. Polly had fallen asleep, and lay wrapped in a towel, a cup of untouched tea just beyond her outstretched hand.

James pulled the duvet over her, and stroked her dark hair out of her eyes. He switched off the lights in the bedroom, and made his way back to the hall, quietly slipping on his drenched parka, and picking up the newspaper. He closed the front door carefully, and made his way down to the street below, taking the stairs two at a time rather than using the clattering old lift.

He turned left on leaving the building, and quickly made his way to Place de l'Estrapade, the little triangular garden to the rear of his building. The park was almost in darkness, the few street lamps failing to penetrate the gloom and the shadows. The streets were deserted, and the sound of the rain falling through the trees and dancing on the pavements was the only accompaniment to his footsteps as he made his way to the small red glow at the back of the gardens.

As he approached, the light from the cigarette glowed a final time and then was extinguished by the figure who stepped out of the shadows.

'Evening Mac', James started. 'Been waiting long?

François Macneil flashed a lopsided grin at James. 'Long enough for my shoes to fill with water. But no matter. You got here OK?'

'Sure. The concert knocked out Polly. She's dead to the world.'

'This was easier when you were on your own, but I know you're good and you're careful. In fact you're quite the celebrity at the Embassy. The officer who killed the Oxford handler. Stabbed him in the neck in cold blood! An actual front line operator. They'll be queuing up to have a look at you when you visit!'

'That was all a bit of a mess as you well know

François. It happened, and I have to live with it, but I'd rather just let it drop now. Look, I have the documents from Hassan. They make interesting reading. There are some names on that list that we've not seen before.'

James handed over the copy of Le Figaro, and François carefully tore a small strip of paper from its middle, where it had been glued in position.

'He's good, isn't he Jamie. And he turned up on time at the usual place?

'Sure. He looked relaxed. I take it that you'll pay him directly?'

'We'll use the usual accounts. You don't need to worry about that side of things. Just continue to be there for him if he does need a shoulder to cry on.'

'Fine. And is there any chance of a more interesting role for me in the not too distant? After all, MI6's latest hitman shouldn't be consigned to lowly messenger work for ever, should he?'

François flashed another of his smiles. 'We'll let you know when to come in for a briefing if there's anything more exciting to do. Don't be impatient. Your time will come but for now, just keep encouraging our friend to shop his dissident colleagues. I know that you're having trouble in your other life because of Mitterrand. Well it's the same on this side of the fence. Since he offered Presidential amnesty to all the bastards we'd banged up in 1980, the streets have been polluted afresh with all manner of ideological maniacs. Mainstream PLO members, followers of our friend Carlos. And now these Lebanese Armed Revolutionary Faction crazies.'

James was amused. 'L.A.R.F.' I'm guessing that they're no laughing matter.'

'I don't understand?'

'It was a joke François. Sorry.'

'Very amusing I'm sure Jamie. Look, thanks for this. See you same time next week. You had better get back up there in case Polly wakens up.'

'Sure. All the best, pal. See you next week.'

James hurried back up to the flat, hung up his coat as carefully and quietly as he could, slipped into the bathroom and quickly undressed. Polly stirred as he drew the duvet over him.

'Jamie? Everything OK?'

'Sure. Just got up to shut the bathroom window. Sorry to disturb you. Go back to sleep.'

He kissed her gently on the forehead and she turned over and back to her dreams of classrooms and concerts.

He lay awake thinking over the events of the day. This was his life. A life in light and in shadow. A double life.

He turned towards the dome of the Panthéon whose ghostly glow filled the room with a spectral light, and he fell into a dreamless sleep.

CHAPTER TWO.
THE INSIDER

James squeezed through the scrum of brokers and made his way towards the back of Traders Cafe where he could see Steve half-hidden from sight in a dark corner.

'Brilliant to see you again Steve. You're looking great!'

Steve hurriedly stuffed a sheaf of documents back into his packed briefcase. 'Christ Jamie! You crept up on me there. Crikey! You're looking the part. Where the hell did you get all that gear? You look quite the urbane young broker. Let's have a coffee - perhaps you'll have more success at attracting the waiter's attention than I've had.'

James called a waiter across at once.

'How's the old gang back in London, Steve? And how are you doing? Still going from strength to strength I'd heard.'

'It's all good. I'm now a senior secretary to a Treasury team working on a big funding programme. Can't say too much as you know, but this is big stuff, and will run for years - assuming Thatcher can cling on to office.'

'Is that why you're here in Paris? Intriguing. Can

you say who you're visiting?'

Steve took a sip of the milky morning coffee, and leant a little closer to James.

'You said to me on the phone that you're doing some research into the nationalisation programme here. I'm involved in something similar - but think of the reverse. Think of the opposite.'

James thought for a moment. Just before Christmas, the government had announced that it was selling off a small pharmaceutical company called Amersham International. The sale was scheduled for next month, and James and most of his colleagues were planning to try to 'stag' the issue - to sell on the first day of dealing, hopefully at a decent profit.

'So are you saying that Amersham is not the last bit of kit that's going to be flogged off? Are you here to drum up support for the sale?'

'You have to think bigger. Think very big. For Thatcher, privatisation is an expression of economic freedom. Popular capitalism, the economic expression of liberty, reducing the State's power, enhancing the power of the people. This is the agenda Jamie, and Amersham is only the start. I'm not saying anything specific here, but to give you a feel for this, I'd direct you to the apparatus over there on the wall behind our less than helpful waiter.'

James peered through the fog of cigarette smoke at the far wall of the cafe, where the battered payphone hung, the wallpaper surrounding it covered by a maze of scribbled phone numbers.

'It's a phone, Steve. So what?'

'Think about it. We're working towards a big announcement in July for a sale in a couple of years.'

A smile began to spread across James's face.

'Christ! I get it. But that will be huge. And I'd hazard a guess that you're here to start building some momentum amongst investors. And as part of that, is it fair to assume that you'll be encouraging them to think of very full valuations for State assets? That they should be willing to pay high prices for State businesses?'

James became more animated as he leant across towards Steve.

'And would it therefore also be safe to assume that Mitterrand's plans will be caught up in all of this? That by the time you've finished hotting up the international investor community, they'll have their sights firmly set on extracting a higher price for their French nationalised stocks?'

Steve leant forward until their heads were nearly touching.

'Well, now we're getting dangerously close to specifics Jamie, and you know I can't go there. I've probably said a little too much already.'

'But you wouldn't disagree if I said the French government will have to pay 10% more than they've quoted.'

Steve sat impassively, his eyes fixed intently on James.

'Or even 15%?', James continued.

Steve continued to sit motionless, his coffee cup held to his lips.

James leaned back. 'I'm guessing they'll have to pay at least 20% more.'

At this, Steve relaxed, smiled, downed the last of his coffee, and began gathering his things.

'Jamie, I always said that you were a clever chap. Now I have some terribly important meetings to attend, so I'll have to dash.'

He winked at James, threw his raincoat over his arm, and with a wave of his bulging briefcase disappeared through the crowd and into the street.

James took a notepad out of his coat pocket and began to make some rough calculations. He scribbled down the prices at which the soon-to-be-nationalised stocks were trading in the six months before it became clear which way the election was going to go. Looking at the numbers, he could make a case for compensation to shareholders of at least 20% more than the values they were currently being offered. And wasn't that a fairer way of dealing with those shareholders? He hurriedly gathered up his things, threw a few francs on the table, and quickly made his way out to the street and back to the Bourse. Now he knew what he was going to say on the call later that afternoon.

'Are we all gathered then, chaps?'

The somewhat ponderous voice of Percival Beloe rang out over the conference phone, which was perched on top of an untidy pile of newspapers and horse-racing magazines on James's desk.

'Are you ready to share your thoughts on the current state of the French policy, Mr. Gunn? We are all ears. As it were'.

'Indeed I am Mr. Beloe. I have sent over a few thoughts in advance via the fax machine.'

'How wonderful!' Beloe exclaimed. 'One of these days I also will master the intricacies of its mysterious technology.'

Then suddenly the strident tones of Marcus Stringer cut in.

'I've read your notes, Gunn, and whether they make sense or not, I am resolutely opposed to making any investment in that hotbed of socialist vice which you currently have the misfortune to inhabit. Our clients would think we were completely fucking mad if we went anywhere near these fucked-up shares.'

Douglas Elgin, the head of strategy tried to refocus on James's report.

'I think you've made some good points actually, James, and thank you for your efforts. I think it would be wrong not to consider your recommendation in more detail. I think we should run the paper up the flagpole and see if it billows in the wind.'

'Bollocks Douglas,' Stringer shot back, 'We are not investing in these fetid shares and that's that.'

Miriam Goldberg, head of research, tried to bring the discussion back to specifics.

'James, I think the numbers add up, and so I wouldn't be as dismissive as Marcus. I like the rational arguments for buying at these depressed prices, but what I can't see is what's motivating the current shareholders, and what pressure they can put on Mitterrand.'

'Well if we can't see how Gunn's recommendation would work, we ought to finish up right now and get on with something more useful,' Stringer barked. 'I think we're done!'

Beloe had sat in silence throughout, but now his very precise voice rang out through the speaker.

'Not quite yet, Mr. Stringer. You see I think we're all failing to ask the obvious question. Why is young Mr. Gunn so confident of his position? Would you say, James, that you have been helped in your research by anyone close to the questions of motivation that Miriam so astutely raised?'

James thought for a moment, before replying,

'I think I've done sufficient due diligence with relevant parties to form a firm opinion.'

There was a long silence, and it became increasingly clear that all were waiting for Beloe to speak. Eventually he cleared his throat and in grave tones began.

'Colleagues. We at Lecrec Proust face a challenge which I would not hesitate to describe as existential. Our capital base has been slowly eroding for some time, and despite all of our efforts, I believe that the firm has only a few months to survive given our current costs. And now we're faced with what I regard as an opportunity to rectify the situation, and before you descend into apoplexy, Marcus, I have been doing my own research into the French nationalisation stocks. I have been putting out feelers around my own orbit of intelligence, and I agree completely with Gunn.

'Our reserves stand at around five million. I spoke to our bank yesterday, and we can gear that up to around fifteen. Then we need to ask the partnership to put up as much as they can personally. That should enable us to go to twenty million. The French Constitutional Council meets to discuss the Nationalisation Bill this weekend and I'm proposing that we ask Gunn to go into the market tomorrow, Wednesday, and invest the lot across the nationalisation stocks.'

Stringer was first to respond.

'Percival - have you had one to many at the City Club? Are you serious?'

'More serious about this than I have been about any investment case for a very long time Marcus. We've always trusted each other, and this time I'm asking you to put your faith in me. And in Gunn.

Take his numbers away and have a ponder, then we'll speak again this evening.'

'You realise that if this goes tits up, then we're finished.'

'And if it doesn't, then we'd make five million between us, which would be a fifty percent gain on our collateral. Douglas, Miriam: views?'

To James's surprise, they were both strongly in favour of the plan. They were only too aware of the firm's creaking financial state, and were happy, on the evidence such as it was, to back him and Beloe.

'I'll call you later James,' Beloe started, 'and give you final instructions. I have every confidence that you'll implement the plan to our satisfaction.'

The line went dead and James found himself staring over the hillock of papers at Pierre, who could barely contain his excitement.

'Jamie! C'est merveilleux! We've never dealt in such numbers before. Did that really just happen, m'Lord?'

James had expected some interest, but not this. 'Looks like we'll have a busy day tomorrow, my old pal. Let's keep this under our chapeaux. Let's pop over to the Vaudeville for a quick livener. But only one, mind. Better keep our wits about us ahead of tomorrow's orders, assuming, that is, that Stringer decides to buy into the plan.'

Two hours later, Pierre was ordering another bottle of Beaujolais as James hurried back excitedly from the phone booth by the cloakroom.

'Right. That's all done. Beloe has confirmed everything. Just one more glass for me, then I'll head back to the beautiful Polly and an early night. The thirteenth tomorrow. Unlucky for some. And if we're right about this plan, it's going to be that lot of smug bastards on the dealing floor whose good fortune is just about to run out.'

The next morning was cold and damp, but at least the rain had stopped for the moment. James rose early, and made toast and coffee and brought the breakfast through to the bedroom while Polly stumbled around the room picking up what she hoped were reasonably fresh bits of clothing from the tangled heap of garments which she called her 'horizontal wardrobe'.

James dressed carefully, his father's regimental tie lending some gravity to his appearance. He went over his strategy for the day one more time; start quietly, diversify the orders, then slowly increase the size and frequency before buying as much as he could as quickly as he could before the other brokers realised that they had collectively sold short in record amounts.

His concentration was broken as Polly pulled on her tights, lost her balance and toppled backwards onto the plate of toast. She laughed as she pulled crumbs and pieces of marmalade out of her hair.

'You are quite mad, you know, Polly' James laughed. Wish me luck today. It's going to be a big one'.

'Why Jamie? What's the story? Have you got some special meetings? Anyone interesting that I would have heard of?'

'No. Nothing like that. Just some broking business that I find fascinating. But as you know, I can be a bit of an anorak'.

'Well I hope it all goes well. See you later for a drink? I thought that we could meet at les Deux Magots and have a bite afterwards at Brasserie Lipp?'

'Sounds great. See you around six.'

As James strolled through the dealing floor towards his office, he nodded greetings to the other brokers. Just another day. No change of routine. No change of demeanour. The list of stocks to buy were inscribed in his mind's eye, along with the amounts that he would commit and his planned purchase strategy. Pierre greeted him with a smile and a softly uttered *'bon chance'*. He was clearly struggling to contain his excitement.

James walked to the edge of the group of brokers as the bell rang for the commencement of the trading session. He held back at first as the brokers dealt with a number of smaller stocks. And then the focus shifted to Rhône Poulenc. James offered a small number of shares, and as usual the price softened until he found buyers. It was the same pattern for trade in Financière de Suez, St.-Gobain and the other nationalisation stocks. Then slowly at first, James began to buy small amounts of each stock. The other brokers assumed that he was attempting to get their prices up so that he could sell more stock, and they happily filled his orders.

Around five minutes from the closing bell, the atmosphere had changed. James had made purchases to fill around half of his orders, and the other brokers were beginning to look uncomfortable. Did he really have demand for the stocks, or was it a bluff? If they offered to sell more - and significantly more - surely he would buckle and scurry back to his office, embarrassed by the overwhelming amount of stock on offer. After all, the value of these shares had been set and limited by the government.

James looked around at the perplexed faces of the brokers. For the most part, these were fairly pompous men, who'd grown complacent over the years. He could see their grasping fingers clutching fat gold pens, poised above their leather dealing books as they looked to one another for some direction, for a lead. And then, as if to compensate for their growing uncertainty, they turned on him with a fresh aggression, yelling huge offers of stock.

Calmly, and inscrutably, James agreed a purchase from each broker. One by one they sold stock in orders which were way beyond their allowed limits. Their selling and James's buying became a frantic cacophony of brutish sounds, and the runners and clerks around the edge of the floor stopped in their daily round of dull routine to watch the spectacle.

And then the bell rang for the end of the session. James walked slowly back to his office. The other brokers looked with concern at each other, and that concern began to take root and grow into a panic as they began to consider a question which they rarely asked themselves: 'what if we are wrong?' Perspiration began to show on their brows as they walked back to their offices, a growing uneasiness hastening their steps.

Pierre was waiting in the office. He could barely contain his excitement.

'Well Jamie - did you do it?'

'All twenty million quid worth. I spent the whole bloody lot. You'd better get on the blower to London and give them the news.'

Suddenly James felt exhausted. He sat down behind his heavy oak desk and shut his eyes. Voices from the floor penetrated his thoughts. The day's turnover had reached a recent record high thanks to him alone and there was a constant buzz of chatter as the market speculated about what was being dubbed the 'British business'. As he left the Bourse that afternoon, he could feel all eyes following his exit, and even as he walked down the grand steps of the market, faces turned to examine him with suspicion. What did he know that they didn't?

He had arranged to call Beloe that evening, and after a couple of very dry martinis at les Deux Magots and the effects of Polly's irrepressible good humour, he felt quite elated as he recounted the day's events from the pay phone in the brasserie lobby. Beloe was understated as ever, but James thought that he detected an unfamiliar hint of nerves in his voice, as he went through the day's orders, line by line.

'So now we have to remain calm and trust in our judgement', Beloe concluded, as James strained to make out his words through the din and clatter of the restaurant.

'We should hear from the Constitutional Council some time on Saturday afternoon', replied James. 'Perhaps we can talk again once we know our fate'.

'Until Saturday, then. And enjoy your dinner James'.

He kept a low profile over the next couple of days, and spent most of his time either with Pierre in Le Vaudeville, or with Polly in the flat or around the Left Bank. When Saturday arrived, he decided to distract himself amongst the venerable bookshelves of Shakespeare and Company, his favourite shop down by the Seine. As he leafed through its treasures, his mind was transported back to his college days, to innocent times amidst the optimism of University life when he had enjoyed the freedom to explore and discuss ideas which weren't his own. The art of dialectic had made him see that politics and social issues were not simple. His own life was certainly far from simple now, and far from innocent, but he hoped that his successors in college were continuing to enjoy those intellectual freedoms.

And it was in the pursuit of those freedoms that he had joined the Service, and had chosen this life of duplicity and half-truths. Even as he moved about his 'normal' life, he maintained a dialogue with himself as he considered his contacts, his planned meetings, the intelligence he hoped to gather, and the threat that his actions were designed to avert.

He would meet Hassan again on Monday. He would provide another link in a chain that would protect lives and frustrate the terrorists and their supporters in the East.

He gazed past the rows of leather-bound volumes towards the river, and was lost in these thoughts as a familiar figure began to take shape in the corner of his vision. Pierre was running along the embankment, waving hysterically, and narrowly avoiding the booksellers who lined the quay. His overcoat billowed behind him, and his face was flushed and animated. This was the work of more than just a Beaujolais too many. He almost fell into the shop, the bell above the door rattling and pealing an erratic welcome. He flung his arms wide in a dramatic gesture, and James waited for him to catch his breath.

'Jamie! You haven't heard? C'est la meilleure nouvelle! The Council meeting has just finished. They've declared that the nationalisation plan is unconstitutional. All the stocks are to be suspended pending a revised bill. Their prices are going to rocket!'

James carefully replaced the early edition of 'The Prince' which he had been studying, and turned to Pierre.

'Let's get Beloe on the line, and then I think that this calls for a toast, don't you?'

'Indeed m'Lord. I think this calls for several!'

CHAPTER THREE.
SUCCESS

James watched the grey blanket of cloud settling over Paris as lights began to stud the buildings of the square in the gloom of the early morning. Monday had come round too quickly after Saturday's news and the party which had followed. Pierre, Polly and her friends had descended on the student union bar, and the celebrations had continued in the flat until Sunday evening. Polly was still asleep as James drank his third coffee and focused on the day ahead.

The stock market would be in a state of some chaos, given the share suspensions, and James was going to be the least popular man in the building given his activities of the previous week. He had arranged with Pierre to use one of the Duberry offices so that he could put some distance between himself and the market noise, and begin to study the emerging government policy.

He was also very anxious to meet with Hassan. Against all the usual protocols, he had called the flat during Sunday afternoon, and Polly had picked up the call before James could vault over the partying bodies to reach the phone. Thankfully,

Polly had paid no attention to the call or the caller. Hassan wanted to change the meeting place, and James quickly scribbled the venue on his shirt cuff, before rejoining the celebrations.

And now here he was in a discreet booth in Café Marly, his back against the wall, and facing the courtyard of the Louvre, so that he could monitor the passers-by. He was early for the meeting. He liked to check a venue carefully; the waiters - did they give him a second glance? The diners and drinkers - did they seem to take a keen interest in him, or, just as suspiciously, take no interest at all?

But Hassan's arrival was as unexceptional as one could have hoped for. He slid into the seat opposite James and beckoned to a waiter. He was, as usual, dressed immaculately, in a light tan overcoat with dark brown velvet lapels, and a starched shirt collar held together under his crimson silk tie by a single gold pin. Small silver- framed reading glasses hung from a silk thread around his neck.

He was dressed as one might expect a wealthy and successful accountant should be in this city of style and elegance. The fashionable set who graced the tables of the Café looked on approvingly. Surely he was one of their own; a wealth manager, a senior manager at Paribas, or Société Générale. James considered how they would choke on their *petit fours* if they knew that Hassan was, in fact, the main financier for the PLO in Paris, their head of money laundering, and in charge of integrating the funds which were sourced from Moscow. He was, James thought, a most unlikely ally.

'Is everything OK Hassan? You sounded a little anxious on the phone yesterday. Why the urgency?'

'You know that I want to help you. And you know that only the most senior members of my Company know about our little chats. And you know that not even our friends in the KGB know about our meetings. It's essential that it stays that way. Have you ever asked yourself why our Russian friends support our cause?'

James moved a little closer to Hassan, put down his coffee cup, and shook his head.

'Because they are cynical bastards. They are happy to help us as long as we appear to use extreme measures. There's nothing they like more than to support terrorists. It's part of their sick way of undermining your society and your values.'

James looked away as a group of diners passed noisily by and took their seats in an adjoining booth. He lowered his voice and turned back to Hassan.

'But you and I know that they've got the wrong measure of you. Isn't that right Hassan?'

A waiter appeared silently at their side and offered more coffee. Hassan waved him away, then smiled and with the slightest of flourishes replied.

'We want to be the good guys. As long as it suits our cause. That's why we want to help you and your French and American friends. And while it's just too complicated to be chatting with the French and Americans directly, you make the perfect go-between. And as it happens, I quite like you in any case James.'

James suppressed a smile. 'I'm flattered I'm sure, Hassan. But seriously, why the urgency?'

'OK. Here's where we are. We understand that Mitterrand is going to visit Israel at the beginning of March. He has suggested to my boss that he will be supportive of the Israelis, but he will also argue that there should be a Palestinian State, and that the Israelis must negotiate with us. All of this is very good for us. It will mark a major step forward in legitimising our cause. It'll give us a seat at the negotiating table. The only problem is the fucking idiots under our umbrella who we can't control. They are proving to be a nightmare. For example, we have information that The Armed Revolutionary Faction are planning a number of strikes against US personnel. And that is exactly the kind of fuck-up that we don't want. We don't want the profile which that would bring. We just can't afford it at the moment. Meanwhile, our Russian friends don't give a damn - in fact they would be delighted if the Revolutionary Faction were as productive and destructive as possible.'

'So what can we do to stop them? What's the plan?'

'Look. Here are more names. These are the bastards who we believe are first in line to take the next assassination jobs. If you can get this to your contacts as soon as possible, then with luck they can be removed from the streets, or otherwise eliminated. We don't really give a fuck how you do it.'

With that, Hassan handed the bill across to James to settle up, and James noticed that he had slipped a neatly typed list of names and addresses under the receipt.

'Lovely to see you, as always Hassan. Take care of yourself, and I'll see that this is taken care of.'

'My dear friend. How nice to do business with one who is so open-minded and so much less judgemental than the average chap. We are all fallen from grace. It's just that some have fallen further, and I'm so glad that you and I agree that there are some who should have further still to fall. We are all unclean James. We are all sinners. But don't you think that sin is relative? I would be the first to acknowledge that our methods have, at times, seemed a little suspect, shall we say. But *he that is without sin amongst you, cast the first stone.* The main thing is that we can trust you and your people to make sure that the names on that list are well and truly eradicated, as soon as possible.'

James watched Hassan as he melted into the group of diners waiting to take their tables, and then was gone. So he was to help a terrorist organisation root out those that they themselves regarded as terrorists. It was a mess, but if it meant that innocent lives could be saved, then it was justified. He smiled as he heard the carefree laughter of the group of students at the next table. But as he walked out towards the Rue de Rivoli he focused his mind. He would go straight to the Hotel de Crillon, where he would call François, whom he hoped would be sitting at his desk in the British Embassy around the corner in the Rue du Faubourg St-Honoré. He hurried through the crowds and through the rain, which was causing a fine haze of mist to rise up from the gardens of the Tuileries.

James looked up at the facade of the hotel. Above the four great stone pillars, cherubs sat on either side of the reclining figure which gazed westwards towards the Champs-Élysées. He had always thought that the modest doorway seemed out of keeping with the grandeur of the building and its sumptuous interior, where he now sat. He had called François from the lobby phone and now he waited for his contact to appear.

François looked flustered as he walked quickly through the lobby, removing his dripping overcoat as he went, showering the assorted staff and tourists along the way.

'I came as soon as I could Jamie. You said on the phone that you've new information from our friend.'

'Indeed François. He was keen that we act on the names on this list as soon as possible. He was as animated as I have seen him.'

'That's extremely helpful, but I have some bad news. A US army officer was shot this morning on his way to his car. The gunman escaped, but it has all the hallmarks of a Lebanese Faction killing. No notice. No warning. It makes this list even more valuable. We'll get on to it straight away.'

James sighed. 'It's getting more and more difficult to keep a step ahead of all these bastards. And it feels a bit depressing to be reduced to taking help from the likes of Hassan, but it's the best we can do.'

François nodded, rising to head back to the Embassy. 'Thanks for the list. Oh, and James, I have a feeling that your wish for a more exciting line of work may be about to be granted. The great man himself will be visiting the Embassy in a few weeks, accompanied by his new second in command. The Chief has elevated your old friend Lucinda Latham to the position of Head of European Operations. And if the rumours are correct, they will want an audience with your good self.'

James was pleased, and couldn't hide it. 'Well I look forward to that immensely, old pal. And in the meantime, we'll keep concentrating on these crazed individuals.'

James watched François's overcoat scatter rain over another group of guests as he left, then turned to the waiter and ordered a French 75. So, he was to be reacquainted with Lucinda Latham. If he was honest with himself, he would admit that she had been in his mind ever since their first meeting. He had tried to enjoy the good fortune that life had bowled at him so far, but there was always a niggling feeling at the back of his mind, that he wouldn't be content until he knew... until he knew what? That they could be a partnership? The cocktail began to sharpen his mind. 'You've enough on your plate without daydreams as well,' he thought to himself. 'Time to concentrate on the day job.'

He drained the champagne flute, and strode back towards the Panthéon.

'Jamie! You're back early!' Polly's voice rang through the flat as James hung up his overcoat, and went into the sitting room.

'My God! You've cleaned the whole place up. It was a complete bomb site when I left this morning. That's great - thanks. And all my laundry has gone, and all the empties and I can actually see the surfaces in the kitchen. This calls for a celebration all over again. Have you been here all day?'

'I popped out for a quick catch up and lunch with some mates over the river, but otherwise it's been a quiet day. What about you. Why're you back so early?'

'It's complicated Polly. I had a couple of meetings, and then decided to come back - there's not a lot to do ahead of the Cabinet meeting on

Wednesday. So where did you eat today?'

'Oh, nowhere special - I don't remember the name of the place. But tell me more about the deal. What happens on Wednesday?'

'Well, that's when the new compensation terms for investors in the nationalised stocks will be announced. And then trading will resume on Thursday. We all sense it'll be good news for us. But just how good we'll have to wait and see. Meanwhile, we should just enjoy ourselves while we wait! I thought we could see a movie tonight. *Reds* is playing in the Latin Quarter. Do you like Diane Keaton and Warren Beatty?'

'Sounds OK, but I've heard from friends that it's a load of predictable right-wing propaganda and Soviet-bashing. Not sure I'm in the mood for that. But if you're really keen then maybe it would be OK.'

'I'm not that fussed Polly. Actually, the other film that I missed recently was *Absence of Malice*'.

Polly suddenly brightened. 'Starring Paul Newman! I think that's our evening plan decided!'

Wednesday arrived and James and Pierre sat in the wood-panelled Leclerc Proust offices, waiting nervously for news of the Cabinet decision.

'Jamie. It's Beloe on the line. Do you want to take line 3?'

Beloe was barely audible through the chattering of voices in the meeting in London, but as James adjusted the volume, his voice became clearer.

'I've gathered the team for a debrief in about half an hour once we've had the decision on compensation. I'll let you lead the meeting. And as you can imagine, there is a modicum of tension and excitement brewing at this end!'

'That all sounds good Mr Beloe.' James replied eagerly. 'Won't be long now.'

Then just as James was putting down the receiver, a commotion began out on the dealing floor which grew in volume as James and Pierre rushed out to find brokers running from the announcements desk back to their offices. A few looked quite ecstatic, but the majority looked like their world had fallen apart around them.

Grabbing the Government notices, James and Pierre returned to the privacy of their office, set up the speakerphone, and James launched the meeting with Beloe and the senior partners.

'I'm going to quote from the official paper which reads as follows:

Regarding the thirty-six banks due to come under State control, the five industrial corporations and the holding companies of two major investment groups, the revised valuation formula has been determined as follows. Prices to be paid in compensation will be calculated on the basis of the average high prices of the stocks in the months between October 1980 and March 1981, before their prices fell. In addition, dividends for 1981 will be paid at a level 14% higher than last year to account for inflation. The expropriated nationalised shareholders will receive bonds in exchange for their shares, which will begin trading on 18th February.

A din of cheering and voices rattled through the speaker, as James turned to Pierre who was making some rough calculations of the effects of the terms.

James called into the speakerphone. 'Can I just have your attention for a moment please. I'm looking at some numbers here which suggest that we should expect gains of up to 25% on our purchases of last week. We'll be able to sell the bonds next month once all of this is settled in law. It's worked out brilliantly.'

Marcus Stringer was first to respond. 'I have to admit to having harboured a little bit of scepticism about this whole bloody adventure, but this news is fantastic. Congratulations to you James, and to Pierre and to you Percival.'

Beloe was elated. 'It was about us all hanging together as a group, Marcus. But however we got here, I'm delighted and not a little relieved by the outcome. Although it has to be said that we've benefitted from the misfortune of the French people. None of these companies are worth 25% more than they were last week. The French taxpayer will ultimately have to pay the extra billions which this exercise in political idealism has cost. But for us, this has been a great success, and I propose that those of us here in London should retire to Garraway's for a bottle or two of something sparkling, and that James and Pierre should do the same. We'll sign off now, but first, can I have a quick private word with you James, before you go?'

Pierre nodded to James, and then set off to set up the drinks at the Vaudeville.

'Are you alone there James?' Beloe's tone was quite jaunty. 'The others have cleared off here. I just wanted to say once again how much I appreciate your work on this project. I think some tangible recompense is deserved, and we are thinking around £30,000.'

James was stunned. 'But that's more than the cost of an average house. It's a fortune. Thank you, Mr. Beloe.'

'With inflation running at 10% I suggest that you spend it quickly,' Beloe chuckled, 'Or buy that average house. I reckon in forty years or so it'll be worth half a million!'

James was delighted but surprised. He hadn't given any thought to what this might mean for him personally.

'Just one last thing,' Beloe continued, 'I had the pleasure of bumping into our good friend Michael Godfrey at our club last week. Of course you probably know him by another name, or even a single letter, if I know anything about the way you chaps work in that other world of yours. Anyway, he happened to say that he would be visiting you in a few weeks, as there's some sort of squall brewing in international waters.

James was intrigued. 'Was he any more explicit than that, Mr. Beloe?'

'Afraid not. He was terribly vague as you might imagine. He seems to think that you might be a useful member of a little team that he's putting together, and asked me about your holiday plans. As per our agreement, I explained that you were, as usual, free to join him on a sabbatical, as it were, the terms of which would be as flexible as he wished or required. In other words, I think that we may not be seeing much of you over the summer. I will create a cover story here as usual. But I'm sure that we'll chat again many times before then.'

'OK. We'll keep in touch. Actually, I had heard that he might be in Paris shortly. Thank you again for everything, Mr. Beloe. And enjoy your evening at Garraway's.'

James closed down the conference call line, then called the flat.

'Polly! Hi there you beautiful nutter! It's time to upgrade that moth-eaten fur coat of yours. I'll see you at the Vaudeville, then it's a trip to the Galeries Lafayette'.

James wiped the condensation off the grimy office window and peered out at the steam rising from the wet pavements. The sun had broken through the clouds and the scene seemed to reflect his sense of elation, not just about the money, but about the thrill of the transaction and its success. He would sell the bonds in February, and then March would bring the meeting with Lucinda and Godfrey. He would be meeting the Chief himself! He wondered what they wanted from him? He was only one of any number of officers handling Middle Eastern agents. That in itself was nothing special. It had to be about something else. Something which was just beginning to develop. He would find out soon enough.

CHAPTER FOUR. THE GATHERING STORM

There was a characteristically understated elegance about the British Embassy. Its three stories of neatly arranged balconies blended into the graceful lines of the adjoining buildings of the fashionable Rue du Faubourg Saint Honoré. Only the Royal coat of arms on the balcony above the high black double doors compromised its anonymity. A single guard stood by the entrance, and on seeing James approach, he spoke briefly into his radio, the doors opened, and he walked under an imposing carving of a lion's head and into the courtyard.

The spring sunshine cast morning shadows on the ancient flagstones, which echoed under his newly polished Oxfords as he made his way to the special operations offices where François had arranged to meet him. As he waited to pass a second security check, he turned over the past month in his mind.

The weeks since the Nationalisation Trade, as his colleagues in London now called it, had passed quickly. He had realised the firm's profits as planned, and as life on the Bourse returned to a more predictable pattern, he'd had more time to focus on his role as go-between for Hassan and his MI6 colleagues, and to speculate increasingly on Godfrey's upcoming visit.

As the weather improved, he and Polly had spent more time around the Luxembourg Gardens, and walking along the banks of the Seine, sometimes enjoying a dinner on the Bateaux Mouches which drifted up and down the river in the weak evening sunshine.

They had enjoyed spending some of James's bonus, mostly on clothes for Polly, but also on dinners and bits and pieces for the flat, including the latest American-style fridge complete with an ice maker for easy cocktail-making. Life was always light-hearted, and they never really discussed issues other than the latest transient news stories. James had tried to get to know her better - what was her family like, what were her ambitions, and, more tentatively, what did she want from a longer-term relationship? But Polly had a way of deflecting the conversation. She didn't get on too well with her parents. There was a suggestion that they might visit one weekend, but that seemed to fall through. Any conversation about the future was foreshortened by discussion of the issues in the present. In truth, if James was honest with himself, it all suited him rather well because he wasn't sure what he wanted from their relationship. He didn't want to get drawn into a conversation about their future, and she seemed perfectly happy with the lack of any sense of commitment between them. It was probably for the best. And if he had been completely candid with himself, he would have acknowledged that today's reacquaintance with Lucinda was a great deal more in his thoughts than he would wish to admit.

James was ushered into a meeting room overlooking the courtyard, and as he took a seat by the window, François arrived and greeted him warmly.

'Just passing through, Jamie. Apparently I'm not required today. Which I guess means that they won't be talking about our Middle Eastern work. I've tried to winkle out some clues for you from the other officers, but it seems to be completely top secret.'

'We're doing a good job with our PLO friends, François,' Jamie replied, 'So I doubt if there'll be any questions or problems about that. In fact, we've seen to quite a few murderous maniacs in the past month. I'll let you know whatever I can after the meeting.'

'Well, I must say you look terribly smart, but is that one of those new power suits? Your shoulder pads are like an American footballer's. What happened to the old Savile Row job?

'Oh just a bit of advice from Polly. You know how it is. Fashion and all that. Not really my thing.'

'Good luck anyway. I think I can hear C's voice

outside - yes that's them now, Jamie. Better scarper. See you later.'

François darted out of the room, and moments later, Michael Godfrey appeared in the doorway. Godfrey, or MG as he was known to those closest to him, or simply as 'C' to those in the Service which he led, cut a reassuringly avuncular figure. His thinning white hair was neatly combed, and below his broad forehead, his heavy black spectacles gave him the air of someone bookish and academic. Not for him, the modish power suit of contemporary fashion, but rather an unremarkable and slightly ill-fitting off-the-peg number, which made James think of the insurance salesman who would visit his family each month. He was studying a notebook, and at first he seemed not to notice James's presence. But then he was striding towards him, hand outstretched, and a lopsided smile forming above his double chin.

'James - a pleasure indeed. It's been several months, and I hear things are going very well.'

'Good to see you again Mr. Godfrey. The last time was in Carlton Gardens.'

James had been so focused on Godfrey's arrival that for a moment he had failed to notice the tall, elegant figure who entered the room silently behind him, and now turned to James. She wore an exquisite Chanel dress, white with black detailing which looked almost military in its crisp sharpness. She laid her briefcase to one side and observed;

'James Gunn. I see your taste in clothes hasn't improved....'

Godfrey hurriedly stepped between Lucinda and James and ushered them to the deep leather armchairs which were arranged around an ornate stone fireplace above which a portrait of the Queen gazed serenely across the room.

'Now let's all relax and have some tea, shall we,' Godfrey suggested, 'I'm sure that our French friends will be able to organise some refreshment while we have our little chat.'

They sat for a moment in silence as Godfrey rang the service bell, and the drinks were ordered. James tried to catch Lucinda's attention, but she was determinedly focused on the portraits of various ambassadors and consuls which lined the walls.

Godfrey fiddled with his pipe for a few minutes, and when he was eventually puffing billows of smoke across the room, he began to explain the reason for their visit.

'James, I had a very interesting chat with my old friend Percival Beloe the other day. You are quite the hero of the hour it would appear, in financial circles at any rate. And the Embassy here is very pleased with your relationship work.'

'Thank you, sir. We had a bit of success in the market last month. But it hasn't deflected me from our work with the local agents. As you'll know, I've struck up a useful relationship with a very senior member of one of our target groups.'

'Quite so. It is clear that you have a winning way when it comes to developing relationships, and that is what I want to explore with you'.

Lucinda had been listening impassively, but at Godfrey's comments she uttered an exasperated sigh, and delving into her crocodile skin briefcase, withdrew a manila folder marked Operation Corporate, and placed it very deliberately on the coffee table between them.

'Ah yes. Thank you, Lucinda,' Godfrey continued, 'Very efficient as always.'
Lucinda returned her gaze to the assorted diplomatic worthies around the walls.

'James, I know that your focus has been on eastern issues, but I wonder if you've paid any attention to recent developments in the western arena? In South America to be precise? You see we would appear to be on a bit of a sticky wicket with our friends the Argentinians. Our Royal Navy contacts are a bit of a lone voice at the moment, but they have a feeling that the tension between our countries which has been bubbling under for some time, could boil over in the very short term. They claim to have intelligence that a group of Argentinian marines are planning to make a very proprietorial and public display in South Georgia Island in the next few days. Here we are in mid-March. By the end of the month, they think that the tension may break out into real hostilities.'

James was surprised. 'That's certainly not on the public's radar. At least, I don't think it is, although like everyone else, I've followed the growing problems over there. The latest Junta seems more repressive than the one before. It's a mess which seems to have no way of improving unless there's a dramatic regime change.'

'But meanwhile,' Godfrey replied, 'the Junta could keep the public distracted and occupied by using the oldest and most cynical trick in the book. A good old-fashioned and popular war. It's clear that Galtieri is under pressure to shift attention from the economic disaster that he and his people have caused. But it's his henchman, Admiral Anaya who has the solution. He is a vocal supporter of returning the Falklands to Argentina, and that could prove to be the perfect pretext for conflict.'

A sharp knock on the door heralded the arrival of the tea. Godfrey picked up the file as the waiters arranged the tea things and hastily retreated.

Godfrey rekindled his pipe, and began to look through the contents. James was intrigued by his comments, but he was unsure what, if anything, any of this had to do with him. Godfrey continued.

'I'm sure you'll understand James, that all of this is, and will remain top secret. No chit-chat to our French hosts, or indeed to anyone for that matter. No slip of the tongue for instance, over morning coffee. Apropos of which, my sources tell me that you are now cohabiting with a young woman.'

'A girl.' Lucinda interjected. 'She's just a kid. A student. How well do you even know her?'

'I'm not sure that her vintage is really particularly relevant, Lucinda,' Godfrey retorted, somewhat impatiently. 'I think I've made my point.'

James was pleasantly intrigued by Lucinda's comments, but was careful to appear puzzled, and answered simply;

'I'm very careful to make sure that my 'other life' remains in the shadows. The friend in question knows nothing of my other activities, I can assure you.'

Godfrey pondered over his pipe for a moment and his gaze settled on James. He was regarded as one of the most effective and popular Chiefs the Service had known. Decisive and resolute with his peers, he was also encouraging and supportive of the junior ranks, and he had that admirable quality of seeming to be at ease with whomever he happened to be addressing. Affable and disarming, his true thoughts were difficult to determine, and right now, James found him utterly inscrutable. Finally, he spoke.

'Good. That all sounds quite satisfactory. I think that we're agreeing that your private life is under control,' and turning back to the folder on his lap he continued, 'and so I want to share with you some of the content of what we will call Operation Corporate. Let's begin by thinking about fish.'

'Fish?' James responded rather dubiously.

'Fish of the flying sort. The Greeks thought that they flew on to the land or into boats to sleep, so they named them "that which lies down outside". On which the Romans based their word for the flying fish - *exocoetus*. Don't you find etymology endlessly fascinating?'

'Completely fascinating, sir. But what does this have to do with the South Atlantic, or indeed, with me?'

'Patience, James. I am getting to the point. The *exocoetus*. It was an obvious step for the technical director at Nord Aviation to name their prototype missile the Exocet when they began to develop it in the late 1960's. Aerospatiale have now been producing the weapons since the early 1970's and the air to sea version, the AM39, has been in operation for around three years. They have been sold widely, and sit in the arsenals of numerous regimes. They are also traded regularly on the black market. And put simply they are a source of extreme concern to us.'

Godfrey paused to take another sip of tea. He replaced his cup very deliberately, and addressing both James and Lucinda, continued.

'To be a little more precise, it's the fact that Argentina is in possession of these missiles which concerns us. They ordered a consignment of ten AM39s through their Naval Purchasing Commission here in Paris, of which five have been delivered. And we know that their air force includes the Super Étendard jets which can carry them into combat. Were we to engage with Argentina, the campaign would have to be based on a naval operation, and our naval boffins believe that at present we are ill-equipped to deal with the threat to our ships posed by these lethal weapons. The concern runs very deep, and may I say, it is already a particular worry within number 10. My own boss, the PM herself, has personally asked me to take charge of developing a strategy around this particular threat.'

James felt both an excitement at becoming party to this most sensitive of information, and also a tension in anticipation of Godfrey's plans. James knew that he would only have been included in this discussion at this stage on a need-to-know basis. Sitting back in his armchair, Godfrey sank into its opulent upholstery. Now his gaze was fixed on the chandelier which was reflecting slivers of light onto the walls and portraits. He continued, as if he were addressing himself.

'Now let's look at this logically. We can't do anything about the five missiles which are already in their possession. Shame, but can't be helped. What about the other five? Well, the PM is already dealing with those through Mitterrand himself. It's a very good thing that he is so in thrall to her. She seems to have that effect on some men. In any case - to the bigger questions. How can the Argentinians get their hands on more missiles? It would seem that there are two routes - the official and the unofficial. With regard to the first, the French have undertaken to delay, dissemble and generally undermine any attempts by regimes which might be acting on behalf of the Argentines, or where the ultimate destination of the weapons is in any way a cause for suspicion. So far so good. But that takes us to the unofficial route.'

Godfrey paused for a moment, and then sitting bolt upright and pointing his pipe at James, he continued.

'And that, James, is why we are here. The black market in arms is, I would imagine, a fairly cut-throat affair, not unlike the trading environment you currently inhabit. It strikes me that the Argentinians will make it known that they are in the market for AM39s and that they will be prepared to pay well over the odds. My idea, and I agree that it's somewhat irregular, is to introduce appropriately experienced officers into the black market posing as arms traders, to make sure that we have as much intelligence as possible on the availability of the goods. And as for you James, I envisage an even more critical role. We understand that the Argentinian operation will be run by Captain Felipe Cortes, who is in control of their purchasing commission here in Avenue Marceau. What I want you to do is to befriend him, use your reputation as a slick trader on the Bourse, and persuade him to let you be his arms buyer.

To be his agent. And that way we can monitor his activities, and make sure of his failure. If you were to get close to actually making a purchase, then you would arrange for the goods to be diverted to one of our RAF bases on completion of the deal. Then you would convince Cortes that there had been a last minute hitch, or that the goods weren't in order.'

James was trying to contain his enthusiasm. This was exactly the sort of work that he'd been waiting for and hoping would come his way. However he managed to remain calm as he responded.

'I would be very keen to take on this role. But if I get close to actually making a purchase, then at some point I will have to show some collateral, or simply produce the cash. I've no idea what these weapons cost, but I assume that we'd be talking about a significant figure.'

Lucinda, who had been listening patiently, and nodding agreement with Godfrey's step by step reasoning, turned to James and in a more earnest tone replied,

'That is a good point James, and as you can imagine, one that we have considered. Now let's be clear, this may all turn out to be very academic. The situation in the South Atlantic may not deteriorate, and we all hope that it doesn't. However, we have to be several steps ahead in our thinking, and so the Treasury has arranged a line of credit in favour of MI6, which we can use at our discretion to purchase goods, if, and it's a big if, it ever came to the scenario you describe. The funds have been signed off at the highest level. I made the arrangements myself with the PM and our people at Williams and Glyn's Bank.'

James was impressed. Lucinda's confident bearing contrasted with the more circumspect character of Godfrey. He thought that they made a beguilingly effective team.

James raised an eyebrow. 'That sounds pretty incredible Lucinda. You are clearly moving in very influential circles. How much is this line of credit may I ask?'

'It's for £16 million, rising, if I deem it prudent, to £30 million. After that, I would have to consult C and the PM. But to be clear, all financial matters go through me. I'm in charge of the money.'

James wondered briefly if Lucinda's show of self-importance was for his benefit, but he replied, 'This must be without precedent. This really is very big.' Then he turned to Godfrey. 'So what are my first steps, sir? How do I set about approaching Cortes?'

'Good question.' Godfrey replied, 'We've decided that you have to get to know him straight away. As Lucinda has said, we hope that this all comes to nothing, but if hostilities commence it would be too late by then to position yourself with Cortes, and so you must start immediately. We have prepared the ground through one of our agents whom we have placed inside their commission. He's been feeding Cortes and his committee details of your work on the Bourse. That's proved to be the absolutely perfect background for creating the persona which you'll now have to adopt in order to gain his confidence. Our agent has added several lines to your CV, which suggest that you have access to an impressive contact list in the arms market, and that you've enjoyed some success in delivering goods to clients. All of which Cortes will be unable to disprove, and unable to resist! And when it comes to actually scouting the market for sources of the missiles themselves, we have a team back in Century House which is researching the market and its participants, so that you should be able to become operational 'on his behalf', straight away if that ever becomes necessary.'

'That all sounds very clear. But what about Beloe and my 'day job'?'

'That's all taken care of. When I lunched with him at the Travellers Club he was in fine form and still glowing about the firm's recent trading profit. We discussed your cover story and agreed that it would be about research. You are taking a couple of months' sabbatical to look more closely at the armaments and aerospace sector. I thought that was apt. Your colleague, Mr. Gavanche, will look after your day-to-day duties. No one will ask any questions. Frankly, you may have more difficulty explaining your new daily routine to your girlfriend!'

'I think the research story will work with her as

well. I'm sure that won't be a problem.'

Godfrey was about to reply when the appearance of one of the private secretaries distracted his attention. Rising from the deeply-upholstered chair he brushed some pipe ash off his waistcoat, and handing the folder back to Lucinda he shook James's hand briskly.

'Must dash James. Very good to see you and I'll let Lucinda fill you in on the details of next steps and that kind of thing. Lucinda and I have to see Mitterrand's people now. Must cement that part of our strategy, although with the PM and Mitterrand both so very much 'on the same page', I don't think we'll have any problems. In any case, Lucinda will keep them right. She'll tell them what they're going to do, and then I'll make them think it was their idea.' He laughed at his own wit as he made his way to the door.

'I've booked a table at Le Train Bleu for the two of you this evening for that further briefing. 8pm, Gare de Lyon. I hope you both have a very pleasant reacquaintance. Now, you lead on Lucinda, and remind me which of these administration people we're meeting first. Goodbye James. I know that you'll do us proud.'

The evening arrangements clearly came as a surprise to Lucinda, who was about to offer some comment in response, but gathered her briefcase, and with a shrug led Godfrey out of the room. James poured the last of the now lukewarm tea. He strode over to the fireplace, and lifting his cup, he winked at the portrait above.

'Wish me luck, your Majesty. I think I'll need it this evening.'

He made his way back through security and into the street where he surveyed the busy crowds and enjoyed the warmth of the sun on his face. He turned Godfrey's words over in his mind. This was why he had joined the Service. If he was called into action, he would make a difference. He would be making history. With a broad smile he looked up at the stone lion and for a moment, he thought that it seemed to smile back at him.

James was changing back into his old Savile Row suit when Polly came clattering through the front door of the flat, laden down by briefcase, rucksack and bags of groceries.

'You're back early, Jamie. What's up?'

'Quite a lot actually', he replied breezily, 'In fact some pretty momentous changes for me. The firm suggested that I take a sabbatical and spend more time researching a specific industry. They want me to look at aerospace and defence.

'Wow! That's amazing! Why are they suggesting that?'

'It's because the trend in broker research is shifting towards specialisation. Analysts looking at more and more specific bits of the market. So I'm a sort of test case. I also think that it's a bit of an additional thank you for the Nationalisation Trades. Beloe is still delighted with all of that.'

Polly was curious to know what it would mean in practical terms. But she seemed satisfied with James's description of a flexible routine in which he floated in and out of libraries, with the occasional meeting here and there with relevant business executives.

'And it might mean the odd trip for site visits - factories, business headquarters - that kind of thing. In fact I'm starting this evening. I have a meeting with a civil servant who works in one of the Whitehall offices. I'll get some background into government policy and spending. I fear that it'll be pretty dry stuff. We're meeting at Le Train Bleu in an hour. Thankfully the excellent wine list should help to alleviate the tedium of the conversation!'

'So, who is he, this government chap? Is it your old friend Steve?'

'Actually, it's a she. I'm not sure exactly which department she's in, but it was suggested to me that I should meet her. Apparently she can help me scope out the research project.'

'So you haven't met her before? And you don't really know what she does? All sounds a bit odd to me Jamie.'

'Not at all. In fact I did meet her a couple of times when I worked in a research institute in London last year, and I think that she was in the Foreign Office then.'

'And does this mysterious woman have a name?'

'Lucinda. She's called Lucinda Latham. Really Polly, it's no big deal! If I didn't know better I'd think that you're a bit jealous!'

Polly dragged one of the bags of food into the kitchen and called back as she went.

'Don't be ridiculous Jamie. You go and enjoy your delicious dinner at the glamorous Train Bleu. I'll be just fine here munching my beans on toast. I suppose Miss Latham is a dumpy dried out old bureaucrat, so good luck to you.'

James didn't respond as he selected his most expensive silk tie, wound the Liberty print into a Windsor knot, and with a brief 'see you later!', slipped out into the evening sunshine.

The sun was fading over the Natural History Museum as James walked briskly across the Pont d'Austerlitz, and towards the looming edifice of the Gare de Lyon. He felt oddly self-conscious as he ascended the curved stairs to the restaurant's imposing arched entrance. He checked his tie in the mirrored hallway as he made his way to the sumptuous dining rooms above.

He marvelled at the ornate carvings and painted scenes of the Côte d'Azur as he was led through the dining room. The old station buffet was like no other. It epitomised the flamboyance of the Belle Époque. The impeccably-attired head waiter led him between the ranks of banquettes to where the room opened out, and to his right he could see the sun beginning to set over the Place Louis-Armand. He looked around for Lucinda and then he spotted her, silhouetted against the yellows and reds of the evening sky. She was sitting with her back to the window, studying the menu, in one of the few tables for two which were placed discreetly back from the clatter and bustle of the main dining room.

James stopped: she looked stunning. Her suit was beautifully tailored and her elegant silk shirt stopped it from being overly business-like. She wore a simple gold Albert as a necklace, and as she held out her hand to offer a very formal, and (James felt) a somewhat awkward handshake, James noted a gold signet ring sporting the family crest.

She had ordered champagne, and as the waiter filled their glasses, they concentrated on the menu while James thought of how to break the ice.

'It was really good to see you again today, Lucinda. You're looking great. And I heard about your promotion. Many congratulations.'

'We might have to work on Operation Corporate together, James. So it's good that I'm not lumbered with a complete stranger or a novice. I should say that my promotion was welcomed within the Service. When the time comes for C to retire completely to the Travellers Club, then I believe that I am in line to become the first woman Chief. The PM has as much as said so.'

'You mean that you see her regularly? Sounds like she's your best friend.'

'Well actually, we were sharing a late supper last week and she said "in politics, if you want anything said, ask a man. If you want anything done, ask a woman". We get along extremely well.'

'Goodness! You really have risen through the ranks like a meteor. It's fantastic. When I last saw you, back in November, I had no idea that it would turn out like this for you.'

'But then again, James, there were a number of things which didn't turn out as expected after we parted. I went alone for my annual trip to Daddy's house in Barbados, you came here to Paris. And now you're very much not alone!'

James was about to reply when the waiter arrived with the food; steak tartare for Lucinda, snails for James. He wrestled for a moment with the snail tongs, trying as best he could to demonstrate more sophistication than he could muster.

'So. You and Godfrey seem to know a lot about Polly.'

'That is our job, James. In fact there is very little of any consequence which we don't know about your *girlfriend*.'

Lucinda stabbed the yolk on her steak, and avoiding his eyes, she scooped up a large mouthful of the raw meat.

James studied his plate. 'She's a very nice girl

actually. It's not like we're serious or anything. We just have fun.'

'You didn't waste a lot of time, James. In Paris two seconds and suddenly you're shacked up with Miss Airhead 1982.'

James bristled. 'Look! That's totally unfair. She's just a good friend. It's not a major romance or anything.'

James was gesticulating with his snail tongs, and in his agitation the mollusc shot out of the contraption, hitting a passing waiter on the back before rolling under one of the banquettes. Lucinda couldn't suppress her mirth and sat rocking back and forth, as James tried to look nonchalant. Lucinda had brightened up.

'Oh for goodness sake, James. Let's change the subject. Tell me about the day job. Tell me about the Bourse.'

James felt a little piqued on Polly's behalf, but he was relieved to shift the conversation, and entertained Lucinda with the story of his success on the trading floor, and the bizarre and somewhat unlikely life of a Paris broker. The main courses arrived; duck a l'orange for James, a steak for Lucinda. James wondered if it had been anywhere near a grill. He watched the blood ooze onto Lucinda's plate, and feeling more comfortable, asked if there was anyone special in her life.

'Afraid not James. Still very much wedded to the job. I must admit that it would have been good to have had some company in Barbados. Daddy's place is right on the beach, just along from Holetown. He had his new wife with him. She's perfectly nice, but rather boring. There's not a lot of conversation going on there, if you see what I mean. We went round to Sandy Lane most evenings. I spent most of my time studiously avoiding the hordes of bloated American would-be playboys. And the idiotic English, in their tailored shorts and woolly black socks!' She shuddered at the memory.

James couldn't help laughing. 'Well, it looks like we might be thrown together if Operation Corporate materialises, and so you'll have my company. I promise to consult you at every juncture on my wardrobe.'

'It could be a lot worse, James. You, I mean. Your wardrobe is beyond redemption.'

As he looked around he saw that the restaurant was nearly empty, and he realised that they had been talking for three hours. Lucinda called for the bill.

'I have to return to London tomorrow, but you'll be briefed at the Embassy about Cortes, your persona and background for the mission, and what your first approach to him should look like. I've assigned François Macneil to be your wing man on this. The two of you work well together. And by the way, I think you'll make a very convincing arms trader.'

James spread out his arms in an exaggerated

show of appreciation. 'Thanks. I'll walk you to the Métro.'

'No need James. My driver will be waiting for me downstairs, but thank you anyway. It's been a good evening.'

With that, she stood and shaking James's hand, she grinned and made her way to the door, her heels ringing out on the polished parquet floor.

James gazed out at the thinning crowd in the square below, and reflected on their evening as he finished his wine. Then he rose, thanked the waiter and made for the street.

'Get a grip James, he thought to himself. 'You're a hardened arms dealer, not a lovesick teenager.' He smiled as he walked back towards the river.

'Or maybe you're a bit of both.'

CHAPTER FIVE.
TAKING THE BAIT

James walked down the tree-lined Avenue from the L'Étoile, heading towards the river. François and one of the technology team had dropped him next to l'Arc de Triomphe, and had parked the Embassy car down one of the side streets off the grand boulevard. James had spent the morning being briefed on Cortes, and 'learning his lines' from François.

Fifty-Eight Avenue Marceau was an indistinct and anonymous modern building, very much the poor relation amidst the imposing nineteenth century splendour of the arrondissement. His meeting was at eleven, and he joined a group of office workers as he made for the upper floors. There was a distinct Friday feeling about the place, and the secretaries who crammed into the lift carrying coffees and pastries from the cafe below chatted excitedly about their weekend plans.

The Argentine Military Commission reception was a drab and cramped room, and James picked up a dog-eared copy of *Aero-engine Monthly* and leafed through its pages while the receptionist looked at him suspiciously from time to time. Eventually, he was led into the main meeting room overlooking the Avenue, where the furniture was moderately less tired. Moments later, the door to the inner office opened and Felipe Cortes entered.

'Mr Gunn. Very pleased to meet you. I hear great things about your exploits in the Stock Exchange. You have made quite an impression at the Bourse. A member of our purchasing committee recommended that we meet you.'

'Pleased to be here Mr Cortes. Always happy to meet potential clients.'

They sat at either end of the scuffed wooden table, and Cortes offered James coffee from a percolator which sat on a table by the window. It must have been brewed for breakfast. He took one sip of the bitter mixture and replaced his cup. Cortes was dressed in a dull brown, wide lapelled suit with an unattractive green pinstripe running through the cloth. His kipper tie also bore green and brown stripes, and looked frayed at the end. He was balding, and sported a lank comb-over. His only neatly-groomed feature was his bushy moustache, which had the shape of a scrubbing brush. But the most striking thing about Cortes, James considered, was his pained expression. He tried to look relaxed in James's presence, but this was a man under pressure. He looked as if he had a great weight on his shoulders.

'Mr Gunn. Or may I call you James? I'd like to get right to the point. It has been suggested to me that your expertise extends to more than just trading stocks and shares. Am I correct in thinking that you have contacts in the market for, shall we say, more tangible objects?'

James had been briefed to maintain a reserve initially, and toying with his coffee cup, he answered with a question of his own.

'I thought you wanted to get to the point Mr. Cortes. Perhaps you could tell me what you want. You look as if you're anxious to obtain something from me, and I guess that you have some very specific items in mind.'

For a moment Cortes looked out at the sun glinting on the tops of the trees in the Avenue below, and then seemed to sink into his chair in exhaustion. He lit a small cigar and drew on it with a resigned air.

'All right, Mr. Gunn. You're correct. I don't have time to play around. I suppose there's no harm in my confiding in you. What have I got to lose? The black market in arms already knows what I'm shopping for. I assume you know of the AM39 and what it can do? The damage it can wreak? I need to find these missiles. I've already been double-crossed once, and I'm now under a lot of pressure to perform. You have the right contacts. You know where I can get my hands on exactly what we need. You can help me.'

He paused and looked away before continuing.

'The only trouble is that you're a Brit. If it

happened that our governments were to come to blows, how would you feel about that?'

James looked straight at Cortes, and replied very slowly.

'If I can help you, and I think I can, then I would be doing it for the money. It really is as simple as that. I'm willing to act as agent for whoever pays most.'

'But what if you're successful and I use these weapons against your own forces? How would you live with that?'

'I've told you. I am interested in my commission. Nothing more. If I was to think about how these weapons are used, I would never organise a trade again. You can think of me as a callous bastard, but that's my problem to deal with, Mr. Cortes. Now do you want to talk about what's important or waste more time discussing ethics?'

'How do you mean?'

'How much are you willing to pay? The market for an AM 39 is currently just under half a million dollars. What would you stretch to?'

Cortes looked both anxious and relieved at the same time.

'I'll go to a million dollars apiece. I need these damned things, and I need them now. What kind of commission would you charge?'

'I would expect a ten percent cut. But if I'm really successful, and can arrange delivery of, say, more than five missiles, then I would take twenty percent on the lot. It's a sort of little incentive scheme, you see.'

Cortes looked pained, but answered quickly.

'All right. I want you on my side. Ten percent and I'll pay more if you find more.'

James rose and held out his hand. Cortes's palm was damp and his handshake was limp. He stubbed out his cigar, forced a weak smile below his thick moustache, and handed James a small file.

'We have a deal. Here are our contact details, and those of our bank. We have a longstanding relationship with the Banco Dolcetto in Rome. You will need to show some collateral if you get close to a purchase. You get in touch with me, and with the people in that file, and we can arrange to show a seller the money.'

'Very good, Mr. Cortes. It will be a pleasure doing business with you. I will start to put out the word with my contacts right away.'

'Yes. The sooner the better. You will see something on your television later which might give you an insight into my haste. The Argentinian flag will be flying over South Georgia Island by the end of today.'

Cortes saw him to the lift, and then hurried back to his office.

Back in the sunshine James walked quickly through the crowds, to where François was waiting. He slipped into the back of the Mercedes.

'That was brilliant.' François exclaimed. 'He's in

such a hurry he just wanted to believe everything about you that we'd fed him.'

'What do you mean? Oh I see, did you…?'

'Yes. Our tech colleagues made a visit to number 58 last week. The whole place is bugged. I loved the callous bastard bit.'

'I'm glad I passed your audition, François. And what about his comments about South Georgia?'

'Already passed that up the chain. This is not looking good. It looks like C's intelligence is going to be proved spot-on.'

James looked out at the cafes and shops as they sped along the river towards the Place de la Concorde. Cortes had taken the bait easily. The difficult part was still to come. The teams back in London would now be monitoring the market for any Exocets which were on offer. As Cortes's man, he would have to front up to the sellers. And meanwhile, it seemed like the Argentinian Junta was on a course which would force the hand of the British government. The sun dipped behind a cloud, casting a long shadow over L' Hôtel des Invalides, and it was with a sense of foreboding that James gazed out at the Musée de l'Armée as the Mercedes swept towards the Embassy.

CHAPTER SIX. INVASION

Two weeks passed without incident. James met Hassan very briefly at Café Marly, but he had no more names for him to pursue. Hassan was worried that a cell of the Revolutionary Faction had gone to ground and was proving difficult to unearth.

James was finding that explaining his movements to Polly was becoming more challenging, especially as she seemed to be there every time he looked round. He started to use the Leclerc office as a means of escape and as a base from which he could quickly be with Cortes or with François, if he was needed by either of them.

It was Friday afternoon. Pierre had made an early exit to the Vaudeville for his customary Friday lunch marathon. James was idly leafing through some accounts in a half-hearted attempt to live up to his cover story. The word from François was that an invasion of the Falklands seemed very unlikely. But James hadn't had contact with him for forty-eight hours, which was unusual, and troubling.

Suddenly the battered door of the office burst open, and James thought it might part company with its hinges. Pierre appeared in the doorway, flushed and clearly struggling to catch his breath.

'Have you heard the news, m'Lord? It's all round the restaurant. C'est vraiment mauvais. Apparently the Argentines have landed in Port Stanley. The garrison is overrun and the Governor has surrendered. The Argentine flag is flying over Government House!'

Just then the phone rang. It was François.

'Don't like to call you on this number Jamie, but you better get your ass over to the Embassy ASAP. Won't say any more just now, but do you have your passport with you?'

'Sure, it's here in the office. See you in thirty minutes.'

Pierre was concerned and a little confused.

'What does this mean, Jamie? C'est sûrement difficile. These islands are at the other side of the world. What can your government do about it? It must be the end of the story before it's even begun.'

'We shall see, Pierre. I wouldn't be too pessimistic if I were you.' James started rummaging in the drawers of his desk for his passport.

'I'm glad you popped in, as I've just had some bad news. I may have to be away for a few days to see an old relative who's been taken ill suddenly. He's in London and it's a lot easier for me to visit than for the ageing parents to come down from Scotland. I can continue my research over there, so it doesn't make a lot of difference to my sabbatical work. I'll see you soon.'

James gathered up his briefcase and passport and with a hasty goodbye to Pierre, ran towards the Métro.

He passed quickly through security at the Embassy, and met François in the Ambassador's office. The room was full of intelligence officers, and several men in naval uniform. Most were on the phones which had been arranged along one wall, while others were consulting maps of the South Atlantic which were laid out on hastily erected tables. François led James to a corner by one of the windows which looked out onto the courtyard below.

'Things have moved so fast, Jamie. Reports began to come in a couple of days ago that there was a military build-up just off the islands. The cabinet has been taken by surprise. There's a real uncertainty about what to do next. The PM has briefed Parsons, our man at the UN, to try to call an urgent meeting of the Security Council. We need to know that we'd have UN backing for any military action if that's the way things go. Admiral Leach seems to think that a military operation is achievable and winnable. He's already moved some assets south from Gibraltar and the base in Scotland. They're talking about an emergency meeting of the Commons tomorrow. And they're more worried than ever about these bloody missiles. Have you had any contact with Cortes in the past couple of days?'

'Nothing much. I've been in touch a couple of times, but just to make sure that communication channels are open. It's all very chummy between us.'

'Right. Your instructions are to call him, let him know that you're still his man. That nothing has changed. Then pack an overnight bag and get on the first plane from Orly to London. Latham wants you to check in and take her through the meeting with Cortes in person. And the teams at Century House want to give you the latest intelligence on where the AM39s are most likely to surface. They have a couple of ideas which you may have to pursue. Here's a ticket for the last flight this evening'

'Thanks François. I'm on my way. I'll pack a few things at the flat then head straight out to the airport. When do you think they'll want me to return?'

'It all depends on how this weekend goes. If we are to be at war with Argentina, we'll know by Sunday.'

François turned to the feverish activity behind him, and called back to James.

'Make sure your story for Polly is a good one. We don't want any leaks on this.'

James hailed a cab and set off for the flat. His

call with Cortes had been short. He was more anxious than ever to have first sight of anything James could secure. As the car weaved its way along Rue Soufflot towards the Panthéon, he decided that he would use the same story as he had used with Pierre. The trouble was that Polly was just so damned interested in his life, which was understandable and rather good for his ego, but a little tricky in circumstances like these. And as he had predicted, she was her usual inquisitive self.

'So, who's this sick uncle, Jamie? How come you haven't visited him before and what's the terrible rush? I thought that at least you'd want to wait to see the latest news on the Falklands. It's terrible! It seems to have come out of the blue.'

'Well, we've never really talked much about our families, have we? I think it'll only be for a few days. I'm really doing this as a favour for my parents. It's a lot easier for me to visit him than for them to travel. And his condition is very bad.'

'Maybe I should come with you? It's Friday. I've no lectures tomorrow.'

James hadn't expected this, but then produced his ticket.

'Ah yes, but the thing is, I've already booked my air ticket. Look. I'm on the last flight, and I think I just about got the last seat. Why don't you have a weekend with your pals, and when I get back we'll go out for dinner and I'll spoil you rotten!'

Polly looked at his ticket, and sighed.

'You're right, Jamie. You go and do what you have to, and I'll be waiting for you when you get back.'

She wrapped her arms around his neck and they kissed.

'You're such a busy boy these days. I just love being part of your life.' She smiled up at him. 'We have such a good time. Our relationship is very valuable to me, you know. Maybe I don't always show it.'

He hugged her close and whispered, 'Let's keep this romantic mood warm until I get back. I'll call you when I know what flight I'm on.'

James hurriedly packed, they kissed again, and he was soon out on the street, where François had arranged an Embassy car to take him to the airport. As he set off, Polly was waving him off from the balcony. The car phone's light flashed, and James lifted the receiver. It was François.

'Things are moving at speed. The UN meeting has been arranged for tomorrow. We should know the outcome by late afternoon London time. C has arranged a room for you at the Travellers Club, and you're to meet with him and Latham at Century House in the morning. Next time we speak, we may be at war.'

'How we would take on the Argentines is not clear to me, François. But we'll learn more tomorrow. One thing's for sure. The price of those missiles isn't going down.'

They headed south through the evening traffic, the drab buildings of the suburbs subduing his mood. Doubt and uncertainty descended over him. How many lives depended on the decisions of the next few hours? A sense of responsibility began to weigh heavily as the airport lights became visible on the horizon.

James took a seat by one of the large windows in the coffee room of the Travellers Club, and looked down at the traffic inching its way along Pall Mall. He ordered coffee and eggs Benedict and spread the morning edition of The Times out on the table. Its pages were full of questions and speculation surrounding the Government's next move in the South Atlantic. As François had suggested, the Commons was to meet later in the morning, and the Prime Minister was going to have to account for the apparent lack of intelligence in the lead up to the invasion. It was rumoured that she would back a full-scale military attempt to retake the islands.

He hailed a cab outside the club and asked the driver to take him to 100 Westminster Bridge Road. The driver's knowing smile told James that he, like every other cabbie, tourist guide and KGB agent in the capital, was well aware of London's worst-kept secret, namely the address of the Secret Intelligence Service. As they approached Century House, James wondered, not for the first time, why such a clear target for a terrorist attack was comprised of twenty-two storeys of glass. With a petrol station at its base.

Godfrey's office suite filled most of the west side of the top floor, with views towards Parliament and Whitehall. The reception was unusually busy, and James was offered coffee and ushered into a side room, well away from the 'civilian' visitors. Godfrey's secretaries were adept at maintaining the anonymity of officers like James who were active in the field. He gazed out across the skyline to the river and beyond, and eventually one of the secretaries returned to take him to Godfrey. A large group was just leaving, and James thought that he recognised members of the Cabinet office amongst them. They looked flustered and unhappy.

He found Godfrey hunched over an untidy heap of files. He sat at one end of the long meeting table, and Lucinda stood at the other. Godfrey seemed distracted, whereas Lucinda greeted him with a smile.

'Good to see you, James. Everything under control?'

'All good, Lucinda. It's good to be back.'

Godfrey glanced up noticing James.

'Ah, dear boy. Good to see you. I trust the club is providing a comfortable oasis amidst this welter of stresses and strains. We have just had the most tedious meeting with the worst kind of minor Whitehall pen-pushers. Most tedious indeed. Let's sit over here next to my desk.'

Godfrey indicated a couple of classic Knoll sofas in the corner of the long rectangular office. He sat facing the wall of floor to ceiling windows looking out towards the river. James sat opposite a wall hung with paintings of cities as varied as Cairo, Berlin, Prague and Vienna. He guessed that these were some of the locations where Godfrey had been stationed during his long career.

'I'm afraid that things have deteriorated,' Godfrey began. 'We had good intelligence from our people in Buenos Aires, over a week ago now, that the Argentines were about to make their move. That dim-witted bunch who you just saw leaving the premises were sceptical of our information, and didn't pass it all the way up the chain. And now the opposition will be berating the government, as we speak, about our lack of preparedness.'

Godfrey reached into his breast pocket, produced a silk handkerchief, and proceeded to clean his glasses.

'But frankly, none of this really matters now. And Lucinda certainly put those minor bureaucrats in their place with some extremely direct language. Where did you learn those particularly colourful expletives Lucinda? You never cease to surprise me!'

'You forget, sir, that as part of my training, you insisted that I spend six months as a member of the Senior Service. That stint in the Navy, and my time in a Swiss finishing school, have contributed to the expansion of my vocabulary,' she said with studied seriousness. James suppressed a smile.

Godfrey replaced the heavy black frames, and was refocusing on James.

'Well, as I say, what's done is done. We need to focus on the present. We understand that Foot is going to give his backing to the formation of a Task Force which will set sail for the Falklands on Monday. That is, if Resolution 502 is passed at the UN today. So far, our sources suggest that we'll have no obstacles. And thanks to our recent efforts, Mitterrand is urging support for us in a most impressive manner.'

James was interested in the speculation in the press about the steps which had already been taken.

'*HMS Endurance* is already down there, and Leach ordered *HMS Splendid* out of Scotland several days ago. But the main aircraft carriers, *Invincible* and *Hermes*, will go on Monday if we get the green light. And I have to say, James, that the level of anxiety about the Exocets has gone from high to extreme. You have made contact with Cortes?'

'Indeed, sir. We have a good understanding.'

'Good. And he doesn't suspect that anything is out of the ordinary?'

'Not at all. He's desperate to find these missiles. His bosses are pressing him hard.'

'Good. So, our teams downstairs have been busy rooting around, and they think they've come up with something. Lucinda?'

She reached across Godfrey's desk and picked up a file.

'There's a lot of talk about assets which might come on to the market. A lot of it is just utter rot. But digging down through all the chancers, opportunists and fantasists, our people reckon that there are probably two groups making noises in the market who have some credibility. Unfortunately, the first would be quite difficult to deal with and to intercept. We believe that there's a group within Cortes's own bank who would not be above a little unconventional trading, if you get my drift. The boss of Banco Dolcetto is a guy who's well known to us, a complex character called Roberto Salvini. He's close to Cortes, and he may try to buy the missiles on behalf of a 'front' customer. Perhaps on behalf of Peru for example, although we'd know damn well that the ultimate destination would be Buenos Aires.'

Lucinda turned to the next section of the file.

'And then there's Michele Rigone. Now, he would be a lot easier to deal with, and he's also very much on our radar. You could read his files, if you had a week or two to spare! He's run every sort of illegal racket imaginable over the past twenty years. He's not affiliated to any of the obvious Italian families. He's a loner. And he's successfully played the Sicilian mob off against the Naples lot for decades. The Italian authorities reckon that he's responsible for around fifteen murders of rival mobsters, most of them competing drug dealers. But they've never been able to pin anything on him. Then around five years ago, he decided to 'clean' all his business affairs. He bought a securities firm in Rome, and now he sits behind it and claims to be totally legitimate. We think that he's running down most of his old activities. But the word is that the potential profits from a trade in the AM39 are just too tempting. Our colleagues at GCHQ have some pretty solid evidence that he's been in touch with some of his old contacts in Baghdad. They reckon that they can produce the goods in around a month from now. We'll keep an ear close to the ground and if he gets close to acquiring the missiles, we may have to pay him a visit.'

'And so you see, James,' added Godfrey, 'you may be called into action over the next month or so. For now, I want you to keep close to Cortes, and make him trust that you are doing everything possible to help him.'

One of the phones which sat apart from the others on Godfrey's desk rang, and he picked it up immediately. He listened in silence, then replaced the receiver.

'That was the Commons. All has gone well. The opposition has agreed to military action. Now we just have to wait for the outcome of the UN meeting. We should know by around four pm. James, I don't think we'll need you again today. Why don't you head off, and perhaps Lucinda can update you later when we have some clarity on the vote.'

Lucinda was rearranging the files and preparing for their next meeting. Looking up she added,

'Sure. I can see you later. I'm meeting an old relative for an early supper in Soho. Why don't you join us?'

'Sounds perfect.' James responded.

'OK. Be at Camisa, the deli in Old Compton Street at five thirty.'

He spotted the shop from the end of the street. A row of hams, sausages and onions hanging from the rail above the window advertised the treasure trove of delicacies inside. He was early for his meeting with Lucinda, and once inside, he was impressed by the variety of cheeses and wines that Camisa had to offer. A tall imposing man, dressed impeccably in a pinstripe suit of the type favoured by City gentlemen, was talking loudly to the young man in the apron behind the counter. They were debating the relative merits of olive oils from different regions, and he was drawn to the man's engaging sense of humour and the jokes which he delivered with a hint of an Irish accent. Before long, they were chatting. It so happened that he was also a stockbroker, who knew many of the Leclerc Proust partners. He went on to describe them using a colourful assortment of adjectives, most of which James was certainly not going to be in a position to repeat.

The bell above the door jangled, and Lucinda entered, looking confident and smart in a beautiful trouser suit and cream silk shirt.

'So, you two have already met!' she laughed as she kissed James's new friend on the cheek. 'Uncle Patrick. As bountiful, brawny and bawdy as ever!'

'My darling Lucy. An unutterable pleasure to gaze upon your radiant visage once more! But what are these dark crescents under your delightful mince pies? You've been burning the midnight oil again, you naughty girl. But I don't doubt that it's been in order to keep Great Britannia afloat, and so I forgive you at once. You should eat more meat and vegetables. Let me take you to the Grill Room at The Café Royal and we can gorge ourselves on various bits of animal.'

'Well, only if you let me pay my way.' She turned to James and added, 'I've invited James to join us.'

'Capital idea. James is a very sound chap. A fellow believer in the health benefits of steak and kidney pudding and a glass of porter, I don't doubt. Let's sally forth to the culinary Holy Grail.'

Patrick carefully picked up his bulky bag of cheeses and meats, and, waving his walking cane above his head, marched out into the Soho evening.

Once settled in the mirrored and gilded opulence of the restaurant, Patrick struck up a conversation with the sommelier, who he clearly knew well. Lucinda took the opportunity to brief

James on the latest developments.

'The vote was passed. Ten to One. Only Panama against.'

He took a moment to consider the gravity of the news. 'And what about the other Council members?'

'Russia and China abstained.' Lucinda continued, 'We don't know which way Moscow is leaning at the moment. They seem to be spouting all the predictable rhetoric in favour of Buenos Aires, but we wonder if they really want to get involved. I guess they'll be happy to sit on the sidelines and see how we react, and to see whether we have the military capability to wage a war on the other side of the globe.'

'So how does the resolution actually work?'

'The Council has demanded the immediate withdrawal of the Argentine forces. They won't comply, so we have the right to retake the islands militarily under the right to self-defence under the UN Charter. The instructions from Godfrey are for you to return to Paris tomorrow, and to make sure that you are all over Cortes on Monday when the Task Force sets sail.'

Patrick had finished organising the drinks order, and rejoined the conversation.

'So how have you been, Lucy? You know that you'll always be my favourite niece. Your aunt Kate sends her love and kisses. I assume that her brother, that imbecile father of yours, is still waltzing around the Caribbean with that young lass of his?'

'Actually he isn't. And you shouldn't be so rude about Daddy. He does his best, you know, and what with the estates in Scotland, the investment portfolios and the properties and his speechifying in the Lords, he's a very busy chap.'

'But he doesn't appreciate the most valuable thing that he has. And I'm looking at you Lucy, for the avoidance of any doubt. Does he know for example, that you are walking out with this delightful young man? Does he give a fig about your personal life? Does he even know what you get up to in that 'office' of yours?'

Patrick was winking theatrically at James.

'You know that I can't talk about work, Patrick. Although I'm always grateful for your support when things are getting tricky in the 'office' as you call it.'

And then, as an afterthought she added firmly, 'Oh, and by the way, I am not 'walking out' with James, or anything like it. We are simply colleagues, with no other connection beyond the purely professional.'

Patrick guffawed as he drained his Guinness.

'Methinks the lady protests too much. What say you, James?'

'We're just colleagues, Patrick. And it looks like we may be working more closely together over the next few weeks, and possibly months.'

'That would suit me very well!' Patrick responded, as he asked for the menus. 'I think you make a jolly nice couple, as it happens, and more to the point, it's good to have another Guinness drinker in the family. Just keep me in touch. We don't want to get ahead of ourselves, but I'm happy to walk you down the aisle, my dear, if that oblivious father of yours is too preoccupied.'

Patrick reached across and patted her hand affectionately. Lucinda rolled her eyes.

'Let's look at the menu, Patrick' she replied, 'and let's talk about the real world shall we? James has an early plane to catch tomorrow, and I have to be back at Century House in a couple of hours. What's it to be? The usual? The inner organs of beasts and fowls, as your famous countryman said? Or liver and onions and a bottle of Claret?'

Patrick's attention was now focused entirely on the menu, much to Lucinda's relief. She raised her glass.

'Let's enjoy our supper. And here's to continued success in our current endeavours in Paris, James.'

They raised their glasses to toast James, and the Task Force.

'And here's to you, Lucinda,' James replied. Smiling, he raised his glass. 'Here's to your 'office job' and here's to us.'

The grill room began to fill with early evening diners, and as the wine flowed, and Patrick's anecdotes of life in the stock market became more outrageous, the troubled world outside seemed to recede for a while. James found himself wishing that time could stand still. But he would be back in Paris by tomorrow lunchtime, and then his thoughts would have to turn again to the challenges which awaited him there.

CHAPTER SEVEN.
THE INCIDENT

James and Polly sat under the crimson awning of Fouquet's as the weak spring sunshine washed the buildings of the Champs-Élysées in a yellow light. The ordinariness of the scene contrasted with the dramatic headlines of the papers in the nearby newsagent's stand, which were full of accounts of the British Task Force preparing to leave Portsmouth. The force would arrive in Falkland Island waters in just over two weeks.

James was sure that Polly had been convinced by his account of the trip to London. He had brought his story to life by using Uncle Patrick as a template for his mysterious ailing relative. Thankfully Polly was more interested in making up for their time apart than interrogating him on his visit, and had insisted on joining him on his walk across the city. He had suggested that they stop for drinks at Fouquet's. From here she would head back towards the Sorbonne, and he would be able to cut down along Avenue George V, and then drop in to his meeting with Cortes. As far as Polly was concerned, his destination was the records room at the military museum at Les Invalides.

Polly was wearing her new red leather jacket. 'I love this, Jamie! It was so generous of you!'

'You look great in it, but then you would look good in any old thing. You know, you would look amazing in Princess Diana's latest outfit - I saw it on the front page this morning,' he beamed at her.

'What? That dreadful thing with the lacy collar and the shoulder pads? You must be joking!' She threw her head back and shrieked with laughter.

'I tell you what, Jamie, stay away from fashion and stick to stocks and shares. It's what you do best.'

James laughed. He had to admit that she had a point. He glanced at the clock above the bar. It was almost time to meet Cortes. He handed some francs to Polly, grabbed his briefcase, and they kissed.

'Let's talk about it later. See you this evening at the flat. Enjoy the sunshine a bit longer. Must get on with my research.'

Cortes's office was much busier than usual. The receptionist recognised James and quickly ushered him into the meeting room, much to the annoyance of the other waiting visitors. Cortes appeared almost immediately.

'Mr. Gunn. I am so pleased to see you. I'm glad that you're still in position and operational, unlike your government's Foreign Secretary. I have just heard that Mr. Carrington has resigned, and now it will be Mr. Pym's turn to persuade the Americans to try to lean on my people to withdraw. I can assure you of one thing right now. From my perspective, these diplomatic efforts will come to nothing. We are on a collision course with the British, so I am keener than ever to do business with you. What are you hearing from your contacts?'

James described his potential Italian seller, without naming him. There was simply too much scope to be double-crossed for him to share all of the precious intelligence which he had picked up in London. But thankfully Cortes seemed satisfied that James was on his side, and potentially on to something which would bear fruit.

'I have to go now Mr. Gunn. I have Buenos Aires breathing down my neck every waking moment. Thank you for your words of encouragement. That will help me to keep them at bay for now. It's disappointing that this particular source of the missiles won't be ready to play ball until next month, but the British fleet won't be properly in position for some weeks. And I have to be pragmatic. I will deal with whoever delivers, whenever they can.'

'I will keep you in touch, Mr. Cortes. Nothing will get past me.'

They shook hands, and once again James was surprised and oddly impressed by the ease with which he was able to lie through his teeth to this stressed and nervous wreck of a man. He walked quickly through the reception and back down to the Avenue below, avoiding eye contact with Cortes's colleagues.

James decided to visit the Leclerc office in the Bourse. Pierre was at lunch, and he was catching up with his mail in relative peace when his personal line lit up. He was surprised to hear Hassan's voice.

'I'm sorry to call you like this, Jamie. Is anyone with you?'

'I'm alone, Hassan. Go on.'

'You have to be careful. I told you last month about my fears. Now we know for sure that there's a rogue group out there which we still can't locate and they're dangerous. I have to be particularly careful, but that's nothing new for me. But we think that somehow they've made the connection between us. We may be wrong, and I hope we are, but you have to take extra care.'

James was shocked. They had both been so careful. His mind began to race.

'Do we know how many of them are operating in this cell? I assume they're armed?'

'We think there are four of them. And they have guns, explosives - the lot. The names are on the list I gave you last month; they're the last of that group which we need to eradicate. If they do find you, and you get the chance, then don't worry about contributing to their disappearance in any way you see fit.'

'I'm suitably warned, Hassan. Thanks for the

heads up. Let me know if you want to meet in the next couple of weeks to share your thoughts. You can leave a note at the reception in my apartment block rather than call. Just the time and place.'

'Good luck, James. And good to talk to you. And by the way, we all wish you well with your problems in the South Atlantic. Especially since they don't affect our own interests!'

James replaced the receiver carefully, and considered his situation. He was unarmed and felt vulnerable. Perhaps he should visit the Embassy and ask François and the head of station how best to proceed. He decided to walk back to the flat, staying in the midst of the crowds as best he could, and then tomorrow he would get advice.

Tuesday morning, and a stream of commuters trudged wearily through the early morning drizzle into the open jaws of the Métro. The neon signs around Luxembourg station assaulted the bleary eyes of the travellers, who gritted their teeth and prepared for the crush of bodies on the platform below. James planned to take the Métro to Châtelet and then walk west to the Embassy.

The crowd was ten deep, and the musty smell of damp overcoats filled the air. As if following some well-planned choreography, his fellow passengers shuffled along as one, as each train swallowed another wave of bodies.

James inched forward to the edge of the

platform and the train doors closed in front of him. He shut his eyes against the rush of wind and dust as the train departed. An unnatural silence descended upon the platform, as the passengers studiously avoided eye contact with their neighbours. James thrust his hands into his coat pockets as the whining noise of the next train began to fill the platform. It was then that he felt something sharp in the small of his back, and the slightest pressure against his ribs. He tried to look round, but he was pressed so tightly to the bodies on either side that he couldn't move. Sliding his left arm back as far as he could, he was able to look over his shoulder. And then he saw the man's eyes fixed on his, a look of cold hatred burning in their dark pupils. The noise of the approaching train got louder, and the passengers began to jostle a little for position. James was able to turn a little, and as he did, he felt a damp warmth seep through his shirt and spread along the small of his back. The man was so close to him that he could feel his hot breath on his neck. And then he saw something glint between them, and realised that the man was holding a knife which he was slowly forcing into James's back. The train was approaching fast. The roar of sound increased as the brakes were applied. It was thirty yards away. The man was pressing hard now, and James felt the knife twist, pushing him forward. The train was seconds away. James's attacker made one last lunge forward. He began to feel his body topple forward. A darkness came down over his eyes and his mind froze. When he moved it was with pure instinct. He clasped his fingers around the keys in his right pocket, leaving the longest one protruding like a spike from his fist. In one movement he clasped the assailant with his left hand, and pulled the knife out of his back with a gasp of pain and terror. Then he swung his right fist around. The key entered the attacker's neck just below his right ear. James could feel it lodge like a fish hook under the man's jawbone, and he pulled his head forward, then staggered backwards as the man's body fell forward onto the tracks and disappeared under the train in an instant.

There was a moment of silence as the shocked commuters realised what they had just witnessed, but then the screams arose along the platform as they stared in horror at the nightmarish scene.

The crowd was disoriented, and in the confusion, James made his way back to the street. He staggered onto the pavement, his overcoat pulled tightly around him, waves of pain searing across his back. The drizzle had stopped, and the sky was clearing. He hailed a cab, and asked for the Rue du Faubourg St Honoré. Hassan had warned him about their enemies. He had said there were four. Well, now there were three.

He had almost fainted as he staggered out of the taxi and past the shocked security guards at the Embassy. The knife wound was quite deep, but he was patched up in hospital and sent home in a government car the following afternoon. He was told to rest for a few days, and to be vigilant. François arranged for one of the armed surveillance teams to keep an eye on his apartment block, and to challenge any drivers who lingered for too long around the south side of the Panthéon.

Polly was frantic with worry. James explained that he had been the victim of a simple mugging - one of those horrible and senseless things that can happen to anyone for no reason. The incident seemed to have really unnerved her. She was attentive and caring. She fed him and she poured his drinks, and went out of her way to make him comfortable. The pain-killers made him drowsy for a couple of days, and he would wake to find her holding him in her arms as if someone were threatening to take him from her.

But James was soon back on his feet and determined to be extra vigilant. Polly checked his mail at reception each day as he had asked, but there was no message from Hassan, so he assumed that the remaining Army Faction members were still on the loose.

Then one morning as he was leafing through the pages of The Times, reading an account of the US attempts to mediate in the Falklands, Polly returned with fresh stocks of wine, coffee and bread, and handed him a small envelope.

'Someone dropped that into reception earlier. I haven't looked at it. What were you expecting?'

'Just some stuff from Leclerc Proust. Tax details and the usual payroll advice.'

'What's the latest on the Falklands, Jamie?'

'According to the paper, Alexander Haig has just left Buenos Aires. He delivered a plan to the Junta, which they'll reject unless we agree to cede sovereignty of the islands by the end of the year, which we won't. The diplomatic situation seems pretty hopeless.'

He went out to the balcony and opened the envelope. Inside was a small typed note which said simply - *al-Watan al-Arabi offices. Rue Marbeuf. Thursday, 9 a.m.*

That was tomorrow. Why did Hassan want to meet him at a newspaper office? He hadn't mentioned the name before. He would call François and have it checked out, and if François thought it was safe, he would arrange for an Embassy car to take him across the city in the morning.

That evening over supper James's mind kept wandering to the meeting with Hassan, and whether he would have any news of the other rogue terrorists. With any luck, Hassan and his people had already dealt with them.

'I'm going to get back to my research tomorrow, Polly. I'll be leaving early-ish. Around eight thirty.'

Polly seemed distracted as she gathered up the dinner things. Something wasn't right. He wondered if she'd become bored by their domestic arrangement. Perhaps for her the excitement had gone out of the relationship. He would make time to talk to her after he'd had his meeting with Hassan.

Next day, James dressed carefully, pulling his shirt slowly over the bandaged wound. He reached for some corduroys and his old tweed jacket. He looked at the elbow patches and made a mental note to overhaul his wardrobe. Glancing at his watch he realised that if he didn't get going he would be late. And then he heard a low groaning coming from the kitchen. Polly was lying on the floor, doubled up in pain. She was having difficulty breathing, and was pointing to her stomach.

'What's wrong, Polly? God! You look awful. Here. Let me help.'

He took off his jacket and used it as a pillow, kneeling beside her and encouraging her to describe her symptoms. He managed to help her upright, and she walked with difficulty to the sitting room where she collapsed onto the sofa. James sat with her in his arms for ten minutes, which turned into twenty and he told himself that Hassan would have to wait. Polly seemed to be breathing more easily now. With any luck, she would be well enough for him to leave shortly.

Then the phone rang, and James picked up the receiver and carried it out to the balcony. It was

Hassan.

'James. Where are you? Are you OK? I got your note, and you said nine o'clock. It's nine now. Have you been delayed or did I misunderstand?'

'But you invited me, Hassan. I didn't send any note. Where are you?'

'At the newspaper offices just like you said. What the fuck is going on Jamie? What the....'

James was almost deafened by the sudden chaotic sound which ripped its way down the phone line. And then the line went dead.

'What the hell just happened?' James thought as he walked uncertainly back into the flat, where Polly was now sitting up and seemed to be more composed.

'I'm sorry Jamie. I've messed up your morning. I don't know what happened just now. It just came on so suddenly. I have these awful cramps sometimes. I'll make sure I get checked up at the University health centre.'

'It's OK, Polly. Don't worry about it. I think I'll stay here after all. Glad you're feeling better.'

A few minutes later, the phone rang again. It was François. Polly was making tea and James was able to talk freely.

'Jamie! Thank god you're OK. We've just had a report from the scene - a car bomb right outside those bloody offices you were planning to visit! Scores injured, and amongst them our good friend Hassan. He was incredibly lucky. He's not in a good way, but they say he's going to be all right. The only bit of good news is that we have a witness who's identified the driver of the car. Your problems are reducing bit by bit. With any luck, by the end of today, there will only be two of these crazy bastards left at large.'

'Well, that's one good thing at least. But something doesn't add up about this morning. I guess the important thing is that Hassan is going to be OK. It looks like things are going to get a little quiet on that front for us, but that means we can concentrate on Cortes.'

'Sounds right. The Task Force will rendezvous with our mid-Atlantic destroyers in a couple of days, and the exclusion zone will be maintained from about a week from now. Keep in touch, and keep on top of Cortes. If you need to keep him sweet, you can open up a little more on Rigone. Century House has intelligence which suggests he may have access to the missiles by early May. You should plan to be going out there by around the middle of next month.'

James looked out over the Paris rooftops and reflected on the attacks on him and on Hassan. He had escaped the trap which Hassan's rogue militants had set for the two of them, but he was going to have to keep looking over his shoulder as he played the part of a trader in arms. His first stop tomorrow would be the Embassy, where he would retrieve his Walther PPK from security. He had a bad feeling that he was going to have to use it at some point over the next few weeks.

CHAPTER EIGHT. THE RENDEZVOUS

It had been a long, pleasant and peaceful Sunday. James and Polly had lunched at Le Procope then spent the afternoon enjoying the early May sunshine in the gardens of the Musée Rodin. The days since the Rue Marbeuf bombing had passed quietly. Polly seemed to be more herself, and James waited for further instructions from Century House. In the Falklands, the exclusion zone had been established, and a tense waiting game had ensued.

Rich aromas filled the air as they passed the restaurants which lined the route to the Panthéon. They walked arm-in- arm, and James began to wonder why he had doubted Polly. 'Savour the moment', he thought as they approached the flat.

But his sense of well-being was short-lived. A card waiting for him in reception bore the code mark of Cortes's office, two horizontal lines with an asterisk between them. Cortes wanted to talk to him.

Polly ran a bath while James mixed a couple of daiquiris. He took his onto the balcony along with the telephone, and called Cortes's number. He was put through immediately.

'You won't have heard the news yet, Gunn, but it's a fucking disaster. One of our ships has been badly hit. I don't know how many we've lost. But it'll be a dreadful number. They're telling me that our navy is crippled. I don't think our fleet will leave port again for some time. This means that we have to defeat the British using our air power, and that means missiles. What more can I say? Find your sellers. Find them! There must be someone willing to sell us these fucking things! I can pay more. You have to help me!'

James realised that he had to give Cortes some real hope, otherwise he might drop him and go elsewhere. He would have to show his hand a little more.

'Good timing, Mr. Cortes. As it happens, my Italian source is becoming more confident that he'll have a consignment of AM39s available for delivery very soon. I expect to visit him in Rome in a week. I'm going to deliver the goods, Mr. Cortes. Tell the generals that they can depend on you, because you can depend on me. This is going to work out well.'

'So you'll be in Rome in a week. Good. I must go now, the news is spreading about the attack. Keep me in touch.'

The phone line went dead, and James could hear Polly calling him. He slipped off his jacket and shirt, and picking up the cocktails made his way to the bathroom.

'Did I tell you that I might have to go off for a few days to research some companies on site?'

Polly reached for her drink and pulled him towards the foaming mountain of bubbles.

'Tell me later, Jamie. We're busy right now,' she laughed.

Two days later, James visited François in the incident room at the Embassy. The diplomatic teams were still handling the fallout from the sinking of the *General Belgrano*. In Buenos Aires, Galtieri had dismissed Peru's peace plan, there was widespread condemnation amongst South American countries, and the teams in Paris were busy shoring up European support. The Americans were still backing the British position, which was reassuring. Amongst the military advisers, the anxiety over the ability to defend Exocet air attacks had reached a new level, and François had news from London.

'You have the go-ahead with Rigone. We have an agent in Rome who we've been using to advertise your trading credentials, and Rigone wants to meet you. He says he's almost ready to deliver ten AM39s. Our agent suggested that you meet him in his office, but he's visiting his country estate this weekend and he wants to invite you and your girlfriend to meet over drinks and discuss the price.'

'Good. That fits with what I've been telling

Cortes. Let's see if this Italian really has the goods or whether it's all just talk.'

James turned to the incident room, where a group of officers was huddled round the newswires, then turned back to François with a start.

'Hold on a minute. What do you mean, "with my girlfriend"? Polly knows nothing about any of this!'

'Not her, of course, Jamie. I'm talking about Lucinda Latham. She'll be going with you. She holds the purse strings and C has insisted that she should be looking over your shoulder when you're talking money. The experience could be quite pleasant, I suppose?' he added with a look of studied innocence.

'I hadn't realised that she would actually be involved in operations. I just hope she doesn't get in the bloody way!'

Then as if as an afterthought, François added, 'Just returning to Polly for a moment, we've decided that it's important to provide her with a full and detailed cover story for your trip. We'll provide you with times, addresses, fake air tickets, the lot. As far as she's concerned, you'll be spending the weekend in Cairo.'

'In Cairo!' James exclaimed. 'Why do we have to go to such lengths? She's always bought my home-made excuses and cover stories in the past. Why can't I just be visiting another enfeebled relative?'

François shrugged. 'I don't know, and frankly, I don't really care. These are the orders, James. Just follow them. After all, there are more important things to worry about.'

Just then, the group assembled round the newswires went silent, and James and François joined them. A report was coming in of an attack on a British destroyer. Two Exocets had been fired. The reports were a little unclear, but it looked like one of the missiles had hit its target.

They waited solemnly as the news fed in little by little. The ship was on fire. There were casualties. The ship would have to be abandoned. Their Naval colleagues looked shocked as they assessed the consequences. The loss of *HMS Sheffield* was going to have a profound impact. The reality of the horror of war would be felt back home. The public would be badly shaken up. Morale would be undermined. And the race to acquire the Exocet was going to become even more intense.

Telephone lights began to flash on the operations desks, and suddenly the room was a hive of activity once again. A secretary from operations advanced upon François with memos to check and some instructions to sign off. He dealt swiftly with the papers, but paused over one file, which clearly contained a surprise. He re-read the papers before carefully signing and returning the documents.

'What are you doing tomorrow evening?' His expression gave no clue to his thoughts, but James could sense that François was having to contain his surprise and excitement.

'Wednesday evening? Nothing planned. Why do you ask?'

'Keep it that way. Don't ask any questions. Just be available to come in to the Embassy from late afternoon.'

'Why all the mystery, François. Come on - give me some clues!'

'Can't say much. All I'll say is, I hope you like whisky'.

'Not particularly, as it happens. Are you saying that a fellow Scot will be visiting?'

'I'm saying nothing, Jamie. Look, let's move on. I have the details of your Italian trip here.'

François handed him a file which included airline tickets and contact details for arrival in Italy.

'You fly to Perugia on Friday morning. It's a small airport - no more than a couple of buildings and a bar. The good news is that you and Latham will be chaperoned by Rod Macfarlane and Lukasz Wilotsyn. They're two of the best officers we have in the region. They've been monitoring Rigone's business in Rome, and they know his country place inside out.'

'But won't Rigone have his spies watching us? Won't he be suspicious if we're seen with guys who he might be able to identify as intelligence officers?'

'Quite the opposite. We're betting that Rigone will have guessed that our Government is keen to get its hands on the missiles. If he thinks that you are an independent dealer, who happens to be funded by us, then that will add to your credibility. And as you're going to find out, Macfarlane and Wilotsyn are the perfect duo to make just the right impression.'

'I'm sure you have it all figured out. But what if we run into trouble? I'm more concerned about the two rogue terrorists on my tail than having lunch with the mafia.'

'You picked up your weapon last week, and Latham will be armed, as usual. I don't see any problems that you won't be able to deal with.'

'Let's hope you're right, François. And meanwhile, I'll keep tomorrow free for my 'blind date'.'

The call had come at eleven o'clock, just as James had begun to think that François had been mistaken, or had mixed up his dates. Polly was out with friends from the history faculty, and he had been alone on the balcony reading through the file on Rigone, when he had received the message to come to the Embassy immediately.

He paid the taxi driver, and as he showed his pass to the doorman at the Embassy gates he noticed that an additional group of guards was positioned in the shadows, just inside the entrance. He crossed the courtyard to the ambassador's building, where he handed over his gun as usual to the security team, who accompanied him past the ambassador's rooms to a part of the complex which was unfamiliar to him. He was led through a maze of passages and down several flights of stairs, before being shown into a sparsely furnished, windowless waiting room. He reckoned that he must be in the basement of the building. No one had spoken on the long walk to his cell-like destination, and now he sat in silence, wondering which senior military chief he was going to meet. He had noticed uniforms in the courtyard above, and thought he'd seen maroon berets in the lights from the ambassador's residence. This was probably a final briefing ahead of his trip. But if those were Paras upstairs, it seemed odd that so many of them were required to keep an eye on one of their own, meeting a minor intelligence officer.

He glanced at his watch. It was just past midnight. Who kept such late hours? Why not just see him in the morning? His impatience was beginning to turn into annoyance, when the door opened and he was taken down another corridor to a large guard room. Half a dozen heavily armed soldiers stood in front of large ornately-carved mahogany doors. The senior officer approached James and expertly frisked him, before nodding to the two soldiers by the door, one of whom pressed a buzzer and waited. After a couple of minutes, a light flashed on the wall to the left of the doors, which the guards opened and motioned James to enter.

The doors closed behind him, and at first he could make out very little in the darkness, which contrasted with the harsh neon lighting of the guard room. As his eyes adjusted, he realised that he was in a large, richly-furnished room, which was lined with portraits of military figures and battle scenes from the days of the Empire. In the far corner, he could make out a couple of large high-backed armchairs with a low table between them, on which sat a small reading lamp, a red case with files piled on top, and a bottle of Bells whisky.

He walked slowly towards the light, and then he noticed the large patent leather handbag on the floor between the chairs. She was absorbed in thought, her face partly obscured by one of the files, which she was studying intently. Without a word, she waved him towards the other armchair, pointed at the whisky and an empty glass, and proceeded to refill her own. James did the same. After a few moments she put down the file, reached behind the lamp for a soda syphon, and topped up her glass. He had heard her voice so many times on television, at the despatch box, on the hustings, in interviews. He expected it to be forceful and confident. In fact it was warm and a little tired.

'Mr. Gunn. I am pleased to meet you, and apologies for the late hour. I tend to work through until around three or four. I forget that others keep more conventional hours.'

At first James struggled to connect his thoughts.

But he soon refocused on the moment. He took a large swig of the whisky.

'Very pleased to meet you ma'am. The time's not a problem. I'm sorry, but I'm just a bit surprised. I wasn't expecting this.'

'Well, I don't tend to advertise meetings like this in advance Mr. Gunn. But I wanted to see you briefly as you should know that we think the work you are doing is very important.'

She turned back to the file on her lap.

'I see that you went to Oxford. I went to Oxford as well, but I've never let that hold me back.'

This seemed to amuse her, and she took a sip of whisky.

'And I see that you have been involved in a nasty incident recently. I hope you're fully recovered.'

She paused to turn the pages of the file, before continuing.

'Interesting background. Quite modest. You've done well to get to this point. I do respect that.'

James felt encouraged by her relaxed manner.

'That's very kind, ma'am. I've just tried to make the most of the opportunities that came my way. In fact I count myself really lucky. I went to an old-fashioned Scottish comprehensive. I got a grant to go to university and I worked hard. And now I enjoy having the opportunity to give something back. And hopefully to help save the lives of our boys.'

'If I may say so, you seem refreshingly unselfconscious. I regret the increasing fashion for making everything reflect back to the self. People can be so preoccupied with themselves nowadays that it soon turns into self-obsession! I'm often asked about my background, but like you, I have no hang-ups about it, unlike the intellectual commentators in the south east. You see, when you're actually doing things, you don't have time for hang-ups.'

Her eyes met his through the dim light of the lamp.

'You know, I think that we probably see things the same way. One might regard one's own background as working class, but in my party we have no truck with outmoded Marxist doctrine about class and class warfare. That's not how we see people. For us it's not who you are, who your family is or where you come from that matters, but what you are and what you can do for your country. You know that we're depending on you and your colleagues to stop these deadly weapons falling into enemy hands. After yesterday's dreadful news, we are more concerned than ever that no Exocets find their way to the Argentinians.'

As she sat back in her armchair, James felt that she looked smaller and almost vulnerable.

'Before you arrived, I was writing to the families who lost their boys yesterday. I write to each one, as ultimately I bear the responsibility for sending them into battle. I try to express my gratitude, and that of the whole nation. I try to express my pain and understand theirs. But it just doesn't seem enough. And then I listen to the radio and sometimes I feel that our boys are being let down. I feel that their sacrifice is something a bit distant and abstract to the armchair experts and the commentators. And they question one's motives. But if we hadn't sent our boys into battle, then what would we be allowing? We'd be letting the dictator, and all those who would wish to emulate him, run over us and trample our principles into the ground. I have to remember what is at stake. When you stop a dictator there are always risks, but there are greater risks in *not* stopping a dictator. My generation learned that long ago.'

James nodded in agreement and they sat in silence for a moment. Then she closed the file, placing it neatly on the papers beside her chair.

'I hope you have all that you need to succeed in your mission? I believe that Miss Latham will be accompanying you, so you will be well-supported by one of our brightest stars and a great personal favourite of mine. You're both people of action, which is greatly refreshing to me. I live in a world of endless talk. I put up with it: I don't mind how much my ministers talk as long as they do what I say! And then there are the journalists and the television people. Always asking what failure would look like. Failure? The possibilities don't exist! When we win this war, and we will, the cynics will say that I was guided by political motives. But you know that I am driven by what is right. As I'm sure you are, Mr. Gunn. And I wish you all good fortune in your efforts. We are counting on you.'

She rose straightening her jacket. James hastily got to his feet. Shaking his hand firmly, she gathered another file, sat down and pressed a button on the side of the table.

'Good night, Mr. Gunn. I will be monitoring your progress.'

She turned her attention to the file, and began to read through its contents. James made his way to the door, which opened as he approached.

Five minutes later he was standing in the Rue du Faubourg St. Honore. The street lights cast a yellow glow over the empty streets and pavements, and he reflected on the rendezvous. The PM carried such a weight on her shoulders. And now she had passed some of that weight of responsibility onto his.

CHAPTER NINE. MY BRILLIANT FRIEND

He could just make out the white buildings of Assisi along the slopes of Monte Subasio as the plane banked and levelled in preparation for landing. James leant forward to look down at the patchwork of fields and villages which spread out from Lake Trasimeno in the west to the hilltop town of Montefalco in the east. The sunlight intensified the golds and greens of the Umbrian plain, and as he looked out at the heat haze, he began to regret his decision to wear a heavy business suit. Lucinda closed her copy of *Middlemarch*, and crammed it with some difficulty into her bulging briefcase. James was amused by her efforts.

'How are you enjoying the book, Lucinda? Do you see yourself as a Dorothea Brooke character?'

She turned to him.

'You mean serious and principled?'

'I meant destined to end up with some dried out old bore like Casaubon.'

Lucinda looked out at the runway flashing past the window.

'That's not how the book ends, as you know

perfectly well.' She turned back to him and smirked. 'But if you think that you're going to emerge as the dashing hero who wins my heart, then think again.'

Put firmly in his place, James gathered his briefcase from the overhead rack, and followed Lucinda down the aircraft steps and onto the tarmac. He paused as he felt the warmth spread across his shoulders and back and the cold, damp winter months seemed like a lifetime ago.

'Get a move on James,' she called back. 'Our contacts will be waiting.'

The plane had been only half full. The other passengers were mostly students returning to the university in Perugia, as well as a handful of seasonal workers arriving to help out with the vegetable harvest, who sat apart at the back of the plane.

They passed quickly through customs, which was no more than a desk manned by two carabinieri, who stamped their passports with a dramatic flourish.

Inside the arrivals shed, baggage was being unloaded from a cart drawn by a tractor. James was gathering their cases when a commotion outside heralded the arrival of a gleaming white Range Rover, which came to an abrupt halt on the parking area, throwing up a cloud of red dust through which emerged the imposing figure of Rod

Macfarlane, followed by the slight, but wiry Lukasz Wilotsyn.

'How absolutely wonderful to see you, James. And Lucinda. It is a great pleasure indeed to meet one of the rising stars of our incomparable Service, and one whose reputation precedes her as the angel Gabriel preceded the arrival of the divinity himself! I am honoured and humbled to stand in your presence!'

He bowed low, and kissed her hand.

Lucinda looked somewhat embarrassed and a little flushed by Macfarlane's effusive welcome, and looked to James for help. But he was clearly enjoying Macfarlane's tendency to hyperbole. Instead, it was Wilotsyn who intervened. He was clutching a clip-board on which he had a carefully planned itinerary, and he was keen for them to move away from the public's gaze. He pressed his wire spectacles firmly onto the bridge of his nose and looked around nervously.

'I think we should be lowering our voices a little Rod. We are becoming a bit of a spectacle. You know that I get very anxious when you are less than discreet. Please, please be a little more circumspect.'

James chuckled to himself. Wilotsyn was only succeeding in drawing even more attention to himself and Macfarlane.

'Oh, buggery bollocks to your boring discretion, Lukasz my old ragazzo! Half of Umbria knows that we're spooks. Spies! Misfits who emerge from the shadows on occasion to prosecute our noble cause!'

He turned to James and Lucinda. 'I say! Let's get you two packed into Lukasz's beautiful motor and get you settled into your rooms at Castello di Monterone before we miss lunch. Signor Piccione, the maestro of wines, has some delicious Sangiovese which he has been keeping for this very occasion, and he has some of the last artichokes of the season, delicious truffles and the finest meats with which he'll create a wonderful culinary concoction. Come along Lucinda and James. Come along. A veritable feast awaits.'

James and Lucinda exchanged quizzical glances before hurrying to catch up with the safari-suited figure of Macfarlane, whose large and muscular frame was already speeding towards the car park.

Wilotsyn eased the car into gear and they set off towards the outskirts of Perugia with Macfarlane bellowing a Puccini aria through the open windows.

James was impressed by the car. It was the latest model, and Wilotsyn's pride and joy. The interior was immaculately maintained, and every dial and switch gleamed as it had done on the day the car left the showroom.

A couple of passengers had been picked up by taxi, but they were soon left way behind in the distance as Wilotsyn pressed his foot to the floor and the Range Rover sped up the narrow twisting roads. After about twenty minutes he made one final veer to the left, and they entered the gates of the Castello di Monterone, one of the most select hotels in the region.

The castle sat on the Assisi to Perugia road, and as Macfarlane explained, it had been used by the Knights Templar in the 13th century to offer protection to Catholic pilgrims.

'A fitting residence for you both, James,' he declared as they carried the bags into reception, 'I'm sure you will love this place, Lucinda, after all the stress and strain of London.'

A number of hotel guests and porters were busily checking and arranging their baggage. Rod pushed his way past the group, and kissing the most senior of the reception staff in a manner which seemed a little over-familiar to James and Lucinda, proceeded to introduce Katharina, the hotel manager.

'Katharina is an absolute darling. She is certainly one of the most efficient and, if I may be so bold, one of the most elegant hoteliers I have had the exquisite privilege to have known. She immediately clicked her fingers and to the consternation of the other guests the porters dropped the bags they were carrying, scooped up James and Lucinda's luggage, and vanished up the great carved staircase which led to the rooms.

'Come along you two. Come along now. I want to show you the views of Perugia from the battlements.'

The view from the castle roof was like a glimpse of a renaissance painting. A small, deep valley separated the ridge on which the castle stood from the slopes leading up to the city. It was covered with perfectly regimented olive trees and vines. They could see the dome of the cathedral, and the great city walls to the south, which seemed to form a balcony overlooking the plain. And to the east, the basilica of Assisi shone in the morning sun. There was no sound other than the occasional ringing of bells from the herd of goats which moved slowly through the trees below. Macfarlane turned to them, and his demeanour was quite changed.

'Look chaps. Sorry about all the nonsense at the airport and again downstairs - all these amateur dramatics must seem a bit over the top. But you see, Lukasz and I were briefed to make sure that you're noticed, so that Rigone's people will associate you with us. Hence all the fuss and noise.'

He squinted against the sun, and loosened his silk cravat before continuing.

'As I understand the current intelligence, Rigone is confident that he can source a consignment of missiles which are bound for Peru. However, he believes that he has a competitor in the shape of Roberto Salvini of the Banco Dolcetto. The word is that Salvini is trying to secure the same consignment on behalf of the Argentinians. I believe that you've met the Argentinian front guy, James?'

'That's correct. Felipe Cortes. He believes that I am shopping for him. But now you mention it, he has talked about Banco Dolcetto to me. And Lucinda, you mentioned quite early in the process that the bank might be getting its hands dirty in the arms market.'

Lucinda was thinking about the impending meeting with Rigone.

'When it comes to tomorrow, what would be the best outcome, Rod? Where do we want to end up with the Italian guy?'

'His intelligence will have suggested that you could be fronting up for the Argentinians. Your meeting here with us will suggest that you might be backed by our government. The best outcome would be to persuade him that you're serious either way, and that you have the money to prove it. I would suggest that you place funds in escrow as a token of your serious intent. Then you'll get his call if he secures the missiles. Meanwhile, we will have to make sure that Century House are trying everything possible to screw up any efforts by Salvini to beat Rigone to the goods.'

Rod checked his watch and with a broad smile exclaimed, 'I say chaps! Lunch calls! We'll eat on the terrace, and we can fill you in on our efforts to expose Signor Rigone for the heartless, crooked bastard that he is.'

Rod was great friends with the chef, and they were soon deep in conversation about which dishes would be best to showcase the region's foods and wines to their guests.

'But first, a taste of the local white wine. Let's push off with a bottle of the Grechetto *per favore*, and then we will sail on with a drop of Orvietto. And while we're savouring the wine, perhaps some eggs with black truffle just to keep our appetites afloat? Oh, yes, and some fried artichokes and anything else that looks enticing.'

James had draped his suit jacket over his chair, and rolled up his sleeves in anticipation of the feast to come. Lucinda was clearly warming to Macfarlane's very genial personality. Lukasz was also neatly dressed in a business suit, and following James's lead, folded his jacket very precisely and placed it on a separate chair. As Rod entertained Lucinda with a history of the castle and the surrounding area, complete with salacious tales of the local residents, Lukasz explained their interest in Rigone to James.

'For years Rigone was primarily of interest to Interpol. We kept an eye on his activities, as there came a time when we thought that his drug deals had involved one of the organised crime syndicates in Moscow. And the Russian mafia do nothing without the KGB knowing about it. We got so close on so many occasions to proving that he had cut a deal with Moscow that it began to become something of an obsession with us. We reckoned that he was being helped by the KGB to launder his drug funds, and in return he was supplying arms to Russian-backed groups in Africa and the Middle East. We were so bloody close. But then he went 'legit'. Sold off his contacts and sources to the next generation of mafia families and bought the Accordia securities business in Rome, a failing brokerage which he now runs as an apparently successful hedge fund. For five years he's been filing tax returns and would seem to be a respectable member of the Rome financial community. The numbers are impressive; it would appear that he's making big profits which he claims are from arbitrage trades. It all looks too good to be true, and it may not surprise you to know that Rod and I think it *is* too good to be true. We think that he's still funded in part by Moscow, and he's using his fake profits and dividends to pay a network of KGB operatives through Swiss bank accounts.'

James leaned back and took a long sip of the chilled wine. He wondered if there was a way to help Lukasz and Rod?

'What do you need to further your research, Lukasz? What would take it to the next level?'

Lukasz drained the last of the Grechetto, as the waiter came forward with another bottle.

'We're working with a private bank in Zurich which is helping us to identify the suspect accounts, but so far we've had no success. Rigone's security arrangements are state of the art. No one is allowed into his personal data system. He employs traders, client-relationship people, back office personnel, and all the other roles that you would expect of a functioning hedge fund. But only he has access to the key accounts. Any light that you can shed on those would help us to break into his business network.'

The *primi* had arrived, plates of tagliatelle with wild boar ragu, which Rod insisted they wash down with some Sangiovese from one of the local vineyards. The sun was at its highest, the wine was flowing freely and Lucinda was animatedly enjoying Rod's company. Next came the tagliata of Chianina beef which was served with a theatrical fanfare, and after consuming a great plateful James thanked their new colleagues and retreated to his room. He had agreed to update François on their progress and to receive any last minute instructions. So he called Paris, then lay on the bed, re-reading the Rigone file once again.

He was woken by the sound of goat bells, and for a moment was completely disoriented. It felt like he hadn't moved for hours. His shirt clung to him, and his mouth was dry. What time was it? Shafts of light shone through the high window of his room, and his watch told him that it was early evening. He showered, then changed into shorts and a polo shirt, and headed out to find Lucinda.

The lunch tables had been cleared and apart from Katharina and a waiter, there was no one around. He walked through the neatly manicured garden to the terrace overlooking the city. Here he found a small plunge pool, and beside it, draped along one of the sun beds was Lucinda, stretched out in a black speedo swimsuit, her face half covered by a pair of very large sunglasses, a martini in one hand, a novel in the other. She spoke without looking up from the pages.

'Wondered when you were going to emerge. Looks like you don't have the stamina to keep up with our hosts.'

'Actually, I wanted to go over the files again. But this heat is a shock and I must admit, I've felt better.'

'Have one of these, James. This'll sort you out.'

Lucinda put down her book, and pressed a service bell. Within moments, the waiter was hovering by her side.

'Another Vesper for my weedy friend please, Luca, and I'll have a top up while you're at it.' She gave him a winning smile.

Luca was clearly eager to please Lucinda, and rushed off to fix the drinks. James sat on the sun bed next to her and tried to focus on the next day.

'When did the guys leave? Did they stay long?'

'They didn't stay much beyond the dolci and a couple of rounds of limoncello. I like them. They're very much more entertaining than your average MI6 spook.'

'And what are the plans for tomorrow?'

'It should be OK if we stick to our cover story, but

this Rigone character is not to be underestimated. According to Rod, he has a lot of blood on his hands. Even today, with his new squeaky-clean image, he's not above causing the occasional permanent disappearance of anyone who gets in his way. Like the accountant who inflated the value of a private company which Accordia bought into last year. Found hanging from the Ponte Cestio in February. Hanging by a blue nylon rope, the same kind of rope that was used to strangle one of Rigone's lawyers last May. In that case the dead guy had made an appointment to visit the financial regulator, but of course he didn't make it, and so we'll never know what he wanted to say.'

'We'll have to make sure that he buys into our story. I hope that our people in Rome have set us up well.'

'We'll be on our own. The plan is for the guys to pick us up tomorrow late morning, then drive us to a bar on the outskirts of Umbertide. We'll leave them there and we'll take Lukasz's Range Rover to Rigone's villa, which is just west of the town, on the slopes of Monte Acuto.'

Luca had arrived with the drinks, and they clinked glasses before James took a hesitant sip of the very dry martini.

'Here's to a successful day tomorrow, Lucinda. I have to say that I'm enjoying this assignment. I'm enjoying being here with you. The boyfriend and girlfriend roles seem to work really well, don't you think? In fact, I was just pondering whether we should promote ourselves to engaged couple?'

Lucinda lowered her sunglasses and for a moment she seemed uncertain of her reply. But then she knocked back her drink, gathered up her novel and towel, and started towards the castle. She stopped at the gates, turned back to James and smiled.

'I'm having a good time too. But we need to focus on tomorrow. An early night for me. And you need to get some beauty sleep. God knows, you need it!'

And with that she disappeared into the castle, leaving James to finish his martini as the sun began to set behind the domes and the walls of Perugia.

It was another blisteringly hot day, unusual for this time of May, and James wound down the window of the Range Rover to gulp in the hot air as they sped north towards Umbertide. The fields on either side of the dual carriageway were a vivid yellow, and here and there great fountains of water fed the crops from the irrigation systems which criss-crossed the Tiber valley. To the east, the sun glinted off the honey-hued stone of ancient hilltop villages. To the west, Monte Tezio's great bulk gave way to the lower slopes of Monte Acuto, the giant cross on its sharp peak clearly visible against the intense blue of the sky.

Lukasz steered them through the outskirts of Umbertide. It was a small bustling market town, yet James noted an enormous, elaborate pink-walled church and a medieval castle complete with moat and battlements. But despite this, the town was absent from the tourist trail.

They crossed the bridge over the Tiber, and as they were leaving the town, he pulled over to the right and parked in front of a small enoteca. Rod seemed as familiar with its chef and the regulars as he was with the kitchen staff at the hotel.

'I think a caffè corretto is required to sharpen our minds. Four of your finest libations please Simone, and don't dawdle. Let's sit here for a moment in the shade.'

James was relieved to get out of the sun. He and Lucinda were wearing their business suits and he felt quite conspicuous amongst the farm workers and builders who were gathered for an early lunch, a couple of whom seemed fascinated by their presence.

Rod explained that they should drive until they reached Polgetto Castle, and then round the base of the mountain before taking the small private road to Rigone's villa. There would be guards stationed along the mountain track, but they had been instructed to let them pass.

'*Buona fortuna*, my friends. We'll be waiting here to take you back to the hotel when you're done.'

James climbed into the driver's seat of the Range Rover, and Lucinda waved as they set off amidst a swarm of scooters and farm trucks.

Minutes later, they were turning onto Rigone's private road, ploughing up great clouds of white dust from the rough, stony surface. As they slowed to take the sharp bends, James could see figures on the hillside to their left. The occasional glint of metal in the sunshine gave away the gunmen positioned amongst the trees above, and as they neared the villa, they could see guards on either side of the gates to the estate. They were smartly dressed in black suits and ties, and would not have looked out of place waiting in a fashionable restaurant, but on closer inspection, the guard who approached James was unshaven, and sported a vivid scar from his ear to the corner of his mouth. It was clear that they were expected. The guard opened the electric gates after a cursory glance and once inside they passed through an ancient olive grove to a small parking area, with steps leading down to what seemed like a very modest building set on the hillside. It might have been a grain store or tobacco tower. To the left, on the other side of the perimeter fence, they could see the movement of sentries on the steep, rocky hillside.

'That's a hell of a lot of security for a fund manager,' James remarked as Lucinda checked the contents of her briefcase. She was feeling a little nervous, as they had decided to leave their weapons with Rod and Lukasz.

'More evidence that he hasn't completely left his old ways behind.' James mused.

They were escorted by a housekeeper past the tower, and then to their surprise an astonishing view suddenly opened out in front of them. Hidden from above and from the hillside, a splendid villa sat below the tower, commanding a stunning view down a long valley which stretched all the way back to Perugia. The building was positioned like a medieval fortress, with broad terraces set high above the valley floor. And standing at the foot of a flight of stone steps was Michele Rigone, dressed casually in a linen suit and shirt, and Gucci loafers. He stepped forward to shake James's hand.

'Mister Gunn! Very good to meet you. I have heard much of your exploits. And I see that you have brought a delightful companion.'

'Buongiorno Signor Rigone. Let me introduce Lucinda Latham. She is my partner, and looks after the financial side of my work'

Rigone moved towards Lucinda, and lingered over their handshake. His eyes remained fixed on her as he motioned them towards the villa.

'Please let me welcome you to my modest country house. Come into the veranda solare and have some refreshment. You must be parched.'

They followed him into a beautifully furnished room where a waitress stood with a tray of cocktails and cold drinks. James was impressed by Rigone's perfect English, which had only the slightest of accents. He was a handsome figure, somewhere in his late fifties, James guessed, but with the athletic build and posture of a younger man. He was impeccably groomed, his small beard looked as if it had been carefully sculpted. He wore the somewhat forced expression of a man who wanted to appear pleasant and relaxed, but was in fact struggling with the pretence. Behind his smile, James detected an impatience and a coldness. He chose a soda water from the tray, and raised his glass in welcome.

'I hope your journey wasn't too onerous. Apologies about all the security people. But as a successful money manager, I can't be too careful. You know how it is with the more sophisticated criminals in this country. One has to be prudent.'

James also selected a soda water, and returned the pleasantries.

'We had a most uneventful journey, thank you. We're very happy to be here, aren't we, Lucinda?'

Lucinda removed her sunglasses and surveying the room added, 'I love your home Signor Rigone. This must be the best view in all of Umbria.'

'Well, thank you Lucinda. And please, call me Michele. Let's drop the formalities.'

Rigone turned to James, but Lucinda could feel his eyes constantly glancing at her.

'Do you know that my name comes from Castel Rigone, where all my family lived for generations. It is a beautiful village overlooking Lake Trasimeno. You must visit it before you leave. But first let me show you round *la mia casa*. I have a feeling that it will surprise you!'

Rigone led them through an opulent drawing room, and past a large kitchen where a team of chefs was hard at work. Incredible aromas filled the corridor which ended with a thick glass door beyond which they could see a large study with views across the valley.

'Only I have access to this part of the house. We may return here if we decide to talk business. But first, let me show you our basement rooms.'

Rigone reached slowly behind Lucinda and pressed a discreetly-positioned switch. A large wall map of Castel Rigone parted to reveal the opening doors of a lift. They stepped in and Rigone pressed the button for the lower floor. When the doors slid open, they were dazzled by the harsh overhead lights and the chill air conditioning of a large dealing room, complete with rows of desks laden with screens and phones. Around a dozen men in chinos and polo shirts were either on the phone or studying the charts which filled the screens.

'We're quiet today. Equity markets are closed, but we still trade currencies over the weekend. You look surprised, James?'

'Good God, Michele. This is amazing. It's the last thing I expected.'

'But I guess you'll be familiar with a lot of this stuff, given your job in Paris.'

'Oh, yes. Very much so. I love the Bourse, the trading and the atmosphere of the place. My work takes up almost all my time.'

'Indeed. I'm sure that it's a fascinating world. But my sources in Rome tell me that you also have some very intriguing interests which fill up the rest of your time. Would that be correct?'

'It's true that I have some very unusual clients, whose interests run far beyond stocks and shares. They are currently in an acquisitive mood. Of course, the main commodity that I deal in is discretion. You are a successful and reputable business man. Any transactions which we might contemplate together would be done with the strictest of security, with complete anonymity guaranteed for all parties.'

Rigone looked pleased and paused for a moment to look at some figures which one of the brokers had brought to his attention. Then he turned back to James and Lucinda, and it was clear that he had finished with social pleasantries.

'We all know why you're here, my friends. Let's say no more until we are in my office.'

Once upstairs, Rigone used a fob key set into his signet ring to open the glass door to his office, which slid aside and closed silently behind them. He adjusted the controls of the electric blinds, causing lines of shadow to fall across the floor and the furniture. He beckoned James and Lucinda to take seats around a low table, which stood to the side of a large custom-made Albini desk, on which was a single monitor. Rigone turned first to James.

'Your reputation as a trader in arms precedes you. I've heard great things about your little black book of clients, and I'm intrigued by the company you keep. Would it be too much to say that you might be talking to either, or both of the parties who, it is said, are so keen to acquire the Exocet missile?'

James sounded assured and deliberate.

'Let me say that my recent conversations with clients have been marked by an increased urgency. Although, as you will appreciate, price is always something which we have to consider carefully.'

Rigone turned to Lucinda. 'And when it comes to price, I should be talking to you?'

Lucinda watched Rigone as his gaze passed over her suit and lingered over her. She drew a calculator and some papers from her briefcase and placed them on the table.

'I am merely the accountant. I keep an eye on our cashflow. On the limits of our trading capacity and on the margins we require.'

'Rigone's mouth curled in what was intended as a smile, but which looked more like a leer. He kept his eyes on Lucinda as he addressed James.

'I have rarely been so intrigued by what you British call a 'bean counter'. You had better be careful, James. I might be tempted to lure Lucinda away from you. Such an attractive woman would make a very enhancing addition to my team. I would love to share a little private time with you,

Lucinda, if that were possible?'

Lucinda remained impassive. She smiled sweetly at Rigone.

'What an extremely charming offer! You clearly have a very enlightened attitude to women in the workplace. But as flattering as your offer is, Signor Rigone, I think we should concentrate on the matter at hand.'

Rigone seemed delighted by Lucinda's response, and his disingenuous smile turned into a smirk, before his face hardened again and he turned to James.

'OK. Let me explain my position. In a previous life, shall we say, I did a great deal of business with some gentlemen in Baghdad. They inform me that our friends the French are considering the sale of a consignment of AM39s to the Peruvian government. Well, it just happens that my Arab friends can intercept this order, and sell ten missiles to me.'

'Sounds interesting, Michele. I'm still listening.'

'Well, then you and I would be in a position to conclude a deal on behalf of your client. Sure, there are others in the market who might think that they can compete with me, but I assure you that my contacts are of the highest quality. You've probably heard rumours about that clown, Salvini, and his ambitions in this regard. My advice is, ignore them. Salvini is an amateur! You deal with me, and you deal with the best.'

He leant back with a self-satisfied look. It was time for James to make his move. He fixed his gaze on Rigone.

'Very well. And so to price. With so many hands to pass through and so many mouths to feed, what would you expect from me?'

'That's simple. One point two million US dollars apiece. I'm being quite open with you. That would yield me a profit of one million dollars for simply having put the deal together. I don't mind being transparent with you, as I don't think you have much choice other than to accept my terms.'

'And if I do, then how would this work? How do you propose to get confidence in my ability to pay, while I can be confident that you won't take my money and then sell the missiles to someone else?'

'I would accept a deposit of twelve million dollars in an escrow account of our mutual approval, the funds to be transferred only once all conditions are met. I give you the list of serial numbers of the missiles that I'm targeting, you can check their provenance against the French manufacturer's lists, then I secure them and take delivery. Then you check them using any specialist you like in a place of my choosing, and then the funds are transferred into one of my accounts. I have three accounts in Switzerland which only I have control over. I use them for personal trades such as this one.'

'It sounds like you have thought of everything,

Michele. It's almost as if you had done this sort of thing before!' James grinned.

'This is a tried and tested route. Trust me on this, James'.

James turned to Lucinda.

'Do we need some time to consider Michele's offer, or do we like what we've heard?'

Their eyes met, and for a moment, they both felt the weight of the decision press on their conscience. What if they were actually to complete this deal? What if it actually happened? Wouldn't that mean more money in the pockets of this vile reptile of a man? Had he really left his past behind? Or would the profit he made from the arms trade find its way into funding more drug deals? That would mean that they were indirectly contributing to the pollution of the streets of every European capital and, to the misery of countless thousands of desperate souls. Or would Rigone's profit be shared with his friends in Moscow, making James and Lucinda complicit in the funding of those who would harm their own colleagues?

Rigone moved to the desk, switched on the monitor, and entered his password. The screen came to life showing a matrix of bank account data. Lucinda glanced at the screen and then back at James. She leaned very close to him and whispered softly,

'I think we both feel the same way about the proposal, James. It's not ideal, but we have to think about what's likely to be the least bad outcome. We know what's at stake on one side of the balance sheet. The other side doesn't look good, but it's not our job to be drawn into a moral debate.'

Rigone was becoming impatient.

'Have you two finished? What's all the discussion about? I thought that we were talking about price and whether you can assure me that you have the funds to meet my terms.'

James stood and joined Rigone in front of the screen and asked Lucinda to join them.

'Relax, Michele. We're OK with the price and we have the funds. We accept your terms, and we're prepared to lodge the collateral now. Is your suggested escrow account one of those accounts on the screen?'

'Exactly, James. You can see four accounts. It's the first one.'

James turned to Lucinda. 'Are you happy to use this bank? Is it on our accredited list?'

Lucinda looked through her papers, and nodded approval. She leaned forward to enter their account data which she had arranged in London. She was about to transfer the funds, when James caught her elbow.

'Just one moment, Lucinda. Let me have your calculator. I just want to double check the currency conversion into dollars.'

They waited patiently as James checked the amount on the screen and tapped out a string of calculations.

'All good, I reckon. Let's go ahead, Lucinda.'

She completed the transfer, and handed a card to Rigone, which detailed a secure phone number linked to an anonymous reception desk at the Embassy in Paris.

'This is how to contact us. You will be able to leave a message with our secretaries and they will find us. Let's hope that we hear from you soon.'

Rigone produced a key from a gold chain on his wrist, and unlocked the desk drawer. He produced a schedule on Aerospatiale-headed notepaper.

'Here are the details of the missiles. You can see the serial numbers, and the manufacture completion dates. The consignment should be ready in two weeks. Three at most.'

James tucked the list into his breast pocket and they shook hands while Lucinda packed her briefcase.

'Well, Michelle, we hope you're successful in intercepting the consignment and we look forward in due course to delivering the missiles to our client.'

Rigone closed the screen, and they made their way back through the villa and into the sunlight. He accompanied them to the car.

James wound down the windows of the Range Rover. Rigone's hollow smile followed them as they turned the car. He was clearly pleased with himself.

'You have certainly lived up to your reputation

James. Take care, both of you. It's in my interests that you both stay safe - at least until we have concluded our business! I'll send a couple of my guys after you to make sure you get down the track safely.'

'*Alla prossima*, Michele. It's been a pleasure.' James replied as he put the car into gear, and they headed towards the opening gates of the estate.

'*It's been a pleasure,*' Lucinda mimicked with some derision. 'The guy is an absolute creep!'

'It's all just business. Forget it. Mind you, I do agree with you. He made my skin crawl.'

The scar-faced guard waved them through the wrought iron gates with an exaggerated flourish, and they began the bumpy ride back along the mountain track. They were elated that the meeting had gone smoothly, and there had been no difficult questions. As they reached the junction with the main road, James stopped the car and looked across at Lucinda.

'Perhaps we could have dinner together this evening to celebrate? Just the two of us. No Rod, no Lukasz. Just you, me and our over-enthusiastic waiter?'

'That would actually be really nice, James. I'd like that a lot.'

She smiled at him, and leaned forward to get her sunglasses from her briefcase. James glanced to the left, just as a scooter rounded the corner and raced down the hill towards them. As it came alongside the Range Rover, James recalled with a start seeing the same scooter with the same two passengers, leaving the enoteca earlier that day. Something didn't feel right. But before he had the chance to move off he became aware of a rush of air behind him, as the scooter passenger leapt towards the car, flung open the rear door and hauled himself onto the back seat. He threw an arm round James's neck slamming his head against the window with a sharp crack.

James managed to put the car into gear and kept his foot to the floor. Lucinda screamed as they raced downhill, his face still pushed against the hot glass of the blood-smeared window.

The Range Rover careered down the road, at first sliding along the metal crash barriers on the left, below which a two hundred foot drop flashed before James's eyes. He was struggling to see through the sweat and blood. The headlights of the car and the bumper ground along the metal barrier, before springing up and smashing into the windscreen, which became an elaborate spider's web of cracks and fissures.

Lucinda screamed as the assailant rammed James's head again against the glass, and turning round, she threw a punch which caught the attacker on the side of his head. He reached into his belt and produce a knife which he drew back in readiness to strike.

'For fuck's sake Jamie! Do something!' Lucinda

screamed. 'He's got a knife!'

James pulled the steering wheel down as hard as he could, and the car veered crazily across the twisting country road before smashing into the rocky mountainside and continuing its erratic course downhill. The passenger door made a rasping noise, and then with a symphony of clattering fell off and spun downhill. In desperation, Lucinda swung her briefcase towards the attacker, just as he made to plunge the knife into James's neck. The knife hit the crocodile skin with a dull thud, and Lucinda was able to push him back, as James wiped the blood from his face and tried desperately to straighten the vehicle.

Suddenly, he was aware of a car behind them. The Alpha Romeo was travelling at speed, and in an instant was alongside the battered Range Rover, forcing James over towards the mountainside. He could see that Lucinda was exposed to the rock walls as they sped downhill. He was going to have to slow the car to a halt.

As he stopped, the mangled bonnet of the Range Rover fell off with a loud clang, and a cloud of steam rose from the engine. For a moment they sat in shocked silence. Then James heard the door of the car open and footsteps approached. He looked round as the rear driver's door was suddenly wrenched open. Slowly the barrel of the shotgun appeared. Then came the deafening sound of the gun being fired. James's ears were ringing in pain, and he looked across at Lucinda who was pinned back, motionless against the dashboard. She was covered in blood. Then he realised that all of what remained of the interior of the Range Rover was smeared with blood and burn marks. A large part of the roof was missing.

He turned back to Lucinda who was rigid with horror. She stared at what remained of the lifeless body of their assailant. James stumbled out and clutching his forehead, he gently helped Lucinda from her seat. She was in shock, and he held her as tightly as he could. He carefully wiped the blood from her face, and they stood together as they faced their rescuers, who had turned their car around, and were about to set off back up the mountain road. The driver's window was wound down, and James recognised the scarred face of Rigone's guard.

'Just a little present from your new friend, Signor Gunn. He means it when he says that he wants you to stay safe!' He laughed, touching his forehead in an exaggerated salute. 'He sends his compliments to you, and to the lady.'

The window closed, the Alpha Romeo screeched into gear and within moments it had vanished from view.

James helped Lucinda to the side of the road, and into the shade of a gorse bush which clung to the rocky surface of the hillside.

'Sit here for a while. I have to tidy up some of this

mess.'

The rear driver's side door came off its hinges easily, and he dragged it across the metal-scarred road, and heaved it over the crash barrier. He heard it smash and tumble its way down into the depths of the ravine, landing with a resounding clash of metal on stone. Then he dragged the corpse by the feet to the same point on the roadside, and, with some difficulty, hauled it over the barrier until its weight pulled it, too, to the bottom of the crevasse, where it landed with a sickening thud.

He looked at the remains of the car. It would be pointless to attempt to clean it. The chassis and body were beyond repair. He turned the ignition key, and to his relief, the engine began to make convulsive sounds of life. Then he took a silk scarf from the damaged briefcase, wrapped it round his forehead, and helped Lucinda back into the car. The colour was returning to her face. She pulled the seatbelt across her stained jacket and forced a smile

'I take it all back, Jamie. Maybe Rigone isn't such a bad guy after all.'

'Actually, I'd say this proves the opposite, Lucy. I wouldn't want to be on the wrong side of him. Look - thanks for saving me back there. I promise I'll buy you a new briefcase when all of this is over.'

The Range Rover stuttered its way back downhill, past Polgetto and then along the final stretch of road to the enoteca. As they approached, they could just make out the figures of Macfarlane and Wilotsyn through the cracked windscreen. The vehicle covered the last few yards then gasped to a halt. A jet of steam was exhaled from its engine, and both front tyres deflated with a long, pathetic hissing sound. Rod rushed to help Lucinda from the wreck.

'Christ! What happened to you? Are you OK? James - your head is a mess! Let's get you inside. My God! Lucinda! What the fuck happened?'

Wilotsyn rushed round to help James, wailing mournfully,

'My car! My baby! It's completely fucking trashed! What the hell did you do to the roof? Where did the bumper go? And the lights and doors? And is that blood over everything? What is this sticky stuff in the back?'

He looked back despondently as he helped James into the cool of the enoteca. James turned to Rod.

'Everything went really well, actually. I mean, apart from almost getting killed. But the meeting with Rigone went perfectly. The money's in escrow, we've got details of the goods that he's planning to acquire for us and he'll let us know when they're delivered. Oh, and Lukasz, sorry about the mess.'

Rod shouted towards the kitchen. 'Simone! Open some wine for God's sake. Let's just calm our nerves for a moment.' The chef poured four glasses, and Rod continued,

'That all sounds excellent. But the car crash. What happened?'

'We were ambushed, Rod. And one of Rigone's guys dealt with our attacker in a very final way. He's at the bottom of the ravine on the Polgetto road.'

Rod turned to Lucinda, who had completely recovered her composure.

'Do you think this is related to the other attacks on James? We'd heard about the car bomb, and then the attack on the Métro. Could the remaining terrorists in the group have followed you here?'

'Of course we'd thought of that. And because of what's been happening in Paris, I asked our people to contact the airline and check the passenger list for our flight. It looks like they messed up badly. And that means there's still one of the gang out there.'

James gratefully accepted the chilled wine.

'Well, look on the bright side, Lucinda. At least that's one less than there were this morning. We got the job done, and that's all that matters. Oh, and Lukasz, I have something which might cheer you up. Something which might compensate a little for your scratched car.'

He picked up Lucinda's briefcase from below the table, and with a sharp tug, pulled the knife from its side. He reached in and produced Lucinda's calculator.

'That's good - it's not been damaged by that maniac.'

He pressed the memory button, and pushed the calculator across the table to Lukasz, who looked at the row of figures.

'I don't get it, James. What is this?'

James handed Lukasz a pen and a notepad from Lucinda's case. 'Write those down quickly while the battery is still OK. We had an opportunity to view Rigone's private bank account details. I pretended to be doing some calculations, but I simply copied down all three account numbers.'

Lukasz was already scribbling down the figures, and with his other hand, he raised his glass to James and Lucinda.

'We'll wait until your deal with Rigone is complete, and then we'll get to work on breaking into these accounts. This is fantastic. Thanks James.'

Rod was beginning to relax.

'In that case I think we ought to have another bottle, and while we're here, I'll ask Simone to rustle up something delicious to prepare you for your flight back to Paris. You already have a sore head, James so another bottle of wine won't make much difference.'

Thankfully, James's cut wasn't too deep, and with the help of the chef and his friends he had been quickly patched up, while Lucinda had borrowed a clean top from one of the waitresses.

She leaned across to adjust the bandage which the waiters had carefully applied to James's wound.

'How're you feeling, Jamie? We should have intercepted those guys. I'm sorry.'

James reached up and held her hand for a moment.

'We're still in one piece, thanks to you. We're one hell of a partnership. I'm actually feeling pretty good,' he grinned.

Rod had returned with some fresh glasses. 'OK you two! Let's get this show on the road. Who's for some Prosecco?'

James settled back and smiled at Lucinda, as they toasted their success and their survival.

CHAPTER TEN. THE SPY WHO CAME IN FROM THE COLD

'So, you just slipped as you were getting out of the taxi?'

Polly carefully peeled back the plaster, and pressed a fresh dressing onto James's forehead. He winced as the antiseptic stung the wound.

'It was a stupid thing, Polly. I just lost my footing and down I went. Anyway. It didn't stop me enjoying the trip. Cairo is a fascinating place. We should go together some time and see it properly. I pretty much just saw the inside of an office and a factory.'

He had already exhausted his cover story in response to Polly's enthusiastic interest in the visit, but now he had to tie up some loose ends at the Embassy, and he was relieved to leave her and her questions behind. He set off into the early summer sunshine, heading north towards the river.

He passed Notre-Dame, and then walked up the Rue de Rivoli towards the Embassy, pausing to admire the window displays at Chanel in Rue Cambon. Perhaps he would return to buy a new briefcase for Lucinda. It would be expensive. And what kind of message would that send? He gazed at the haut couture in the window. What was he doing with Polly? All the lies that he had told her began to weigh on his conscience. Perhaps the relationship made no sense. Perhaps he should be with someone who understood his double life. Perhaps with someone who shared it?

His thoughts were interrupted by an exquisitely-attired member of the Chanel door staff, who asked somewhat pompously if he could be of assistance.

'Sure. When are you having the next sale? Most of the stuff in the window seems a bit overpriced.'

'We don't hold sales, sir. We don't need to. Perhaps this isn't quite the right place for you.'

'Fair enough. It's just that I'm a great friend of the Lathams. I believe that Lord Latham of Argyll and Bute is one of your regular customers? I was tempted by one of your briefcases, but I think the moment has passed.'

The doorman began to mutter some words of apology, but James was already rounding the corner and heading towards the Embassy. What a ridiculous world, he thought, where dropping a name can make such an impact. It was all nonsense of course, but it was also fascinating. He enjoyed learning all the little codes and behaviours which opened the door to 'polite' society. But he knew that in reality he would always be considered an outsider. He was happy with that. It suited him very well.

He was escorted through the security department, the dressing on his forehead drawing some quizzical looks as he went. He made his way to the operations room where he called Cortes, who had been waiting expectantly for news of his trip to Italy. The call went well, and as he was putting down the receiver, François rushed over to greet him, barely suppressing his mirth as he did so.

'You're beginning to make a habit of this Jamie, stumbling across our threshold looking like you've been beaten up.'

'Very amusing. I *was* bloody well beaten up. Didn't you read the report? And how you guys missed those two, God only knows. We were lucky to get out in one piece.'

François was serious for a moment. 'The bad news is that there's no trace of the last one. He must have travelled north towards Arezzo, and then disappeared into the rail system. We're really sorry about that. We've let you down. All a bit of a cock up I'm afraid, Jamie.'

'Well at least the guy's very isolated now. He's on his own. With any luck Hassan's people will hunt him down before he can do any more damage. Or we'll get a clear shot at him ourselves. Anyway - I'm staying focused on the missile deal. It went well with Rigone, and I've just called Cortes to reassure him that I've shaken hands on a consignment of missiles which has better provenance than anything else he's likely to be offered. I impressed on him that he'd be crazy not to stick with us, and that he should hold off making any other deals until we've delivered the ten Exocets. Rigone reckons that he'll be able to conclude the deal by the end of May or earlier. I persuaded Cortes that in under three weeks he'll have what he wants and the pressure will be off him. He's sticking with me.'

'That's excellent news. Will you let London know about Cortes, or will I update C and Latham?'

'You'll be speaking to them in any case, so you do it François. And send my best regards to Latham. I hope she's none the worse for our adventure.'

'Certainly will. From what I've heard, it sounds like it was just as well that she was with you, and that she did get in the way after all!'

James could hear François's laughter as he made his way between the telex machines and banks of phones, before disappearing back into the depths of the Embassy.

The following couple of weeks were tense, as James waited for the call from Rigone to confirm delivery. News from the Falklands was mixed. The QE2 set sail from Southampton carrying 5 Infantry Brigade, and the British press took heart from the scenes and from suggestions that a new diplomatic solution might be achieved.

But as an insider, James was keenly aware of the continuing anxiety about the Exocet threat. From the privileged position of the operations room, he followed the SAS attack on Pebble Island, and the destruction of the Argentinian airborne capability on the site, which served to relieve the tension a little. But in the final week of May, the sinkings of *HMS Antelope* and *HMS Ardent,* were stark reminders of the risk that the British fleet faced. And then the sinkings of *HMS Coventry* and *SS Atlantic Conveyor* sent a renewed wave of frustration and anxiety through the Government, MI6 and the Admiralty.

So James was not surprised when a call from François came on the last day of the month. He and Polly had taken a Sunday stroll among the bouquinistes which lined the Quai Voltaire, and then she had gone to meet friends for a late lunch. James was back at the Panthéon flat when the phone rang.

'James. You have to get over here to the Embassy as quickly as you can. There's been a development. Is Polly with you? Is that going to be difficult?'

'No - she's with friends. I'm on my way. What's happening?'

'I'll let Latham tell you. She's just arrived from London. Her friend the PM has been busy over the past few days, and she thinks there may be a knock-on effect to your deal with Rigone.'

'OK. I'll be with you in thirty minutes.'

James hurriedly paid the cab driver, and was ushered into the large room overlooking the courtyard where he had met Lucinda and Godfrey back in March. Moments later, Lucinda entered, looking rather severe in a black trouser suit and shirt. She smiled as she approached, and shook hands briskly.

'Good to see you. How's the head?'

'It's fine. Good job they didn't hit something important. How are you? No ill effects from our Italian trip?'

Lucinda collapsed into one of the sofas. 'I've had too much to worry about, Jamie. As soon as I returned, Godfrey brought me up to speed with the latest problem we face on the diplomatic front. It seems that Mitterrand was coming under increasing pressure from the Peruvian Government to honour a contract for ten Exocets. He'd been kicking that can down the road for weeks, but eventually he called the PM to say that he didn't think he could put off the transaction any longer.'

James looked out of the high windows onto the courtyard below, where shadows were beginning to lengthen on the cobble stones. 'And we all know what that would mean. They would find their way to the arsenal of the Junta as sure as night follows day.'

'Precisely. And so earlier today the PM called him and got tough. Fulfil this contract and it will have repercussions. She even suggested that our membership and role in NATO might be affected.'

James went over to the drinks cabinet and poured two whiskies. He handed one to Lucinda. 'And how did he react? I thought there was a good understanding between those two.'

Lucinda took a sip of the whisky. 'It's good news. But I think it's complicated. Mitterrand backed down. The relationship with us is just too important for him to jeopardise. And so he called the Peruvians and said that he can't deliver for "political reasons". He was both as vague and at the same time as effective as that.'

'And the complication?' James sat opposite Lucinda and considered the contents of his glass. 'I guess that now we're wondering if that batch of missiles was the same batch as Rigone thought he'd be able to intercept and then sell on to us.'

'That is exactly the point. I thought that I should be here with you so that we can deal with him together if it turns out that Mitterrand has effectively ruined Rigone's plans.'

'I could check the serial numbers of Rigoni's consignment against the missiles that Mitterrand has held up.'

Lucinda moved across to the intercom by the side of the drinks cabinet, and called the chief secretaries' office.

'Could you bring me the file relating to the PM's recent conference? It's marked for A1 and 2 clearance only. Thanks.'

She turned to James, 'And where's the file that Rigone gave us?'

'I left the serial numbers at my flat. We can go there together and see if they match.'

'Won't that be awkward, James? What about your girlfriend?'

'She's out. She was very specific about her plans today, so that won't be a problem.'

There was an uncomfortable silence as James played with his glass, and Lucinda feigned interest in the pigeons outside in the courtyard. It was eventually broken by a sharp knock on the door and the appearance of one of the junior secretaries. He was clearly a little nervous in the presence of C's deputy.

'Terribly sorry to disturb you Miss Latham. Here's the file you requested. And... there's something else.'

Lucinda took the file and began to leaf through its pages. She responded without looking up.

'And are you going to tell me what it is?'

'Yes, of course Miss Latham. It's just that someone has called for you and Mr Gunn. He called on one of the confidential lines and he seems to be extremely annoyed about something.'

'Well hurry back then, and have the call put through here as quickly as possible before he thinks we're totally incompetent.'

The young man seemed pleased to be of further assistance. Lucinda pointed at the door, and he made a swift exit.

'I think we know who this will be. Sounds like he's been let down, but I wonder how much he actually knows?'

The intercom light flashed and Lucinda opened the line. Seconds later, Rigone's voice filled the room.

'Is that you, Gunn? Is this a private line?'

James placed the speaker on the low table between the sofas.

'Michele, it's James here. You're free to talk. I have Lucinda with me. You seem a bit troubled. Is everything OK?'

'No, it fucking well is not! I don't understand what's happening. All I know is that my friends in Baghdad have encountered a problem. They tell me that the consignment is no longer available. They have always been reliable people, so I suspect that someone has intercepted the goods further up the chain. This is embarrassing, James. It's fucking embarrassing.'

James spoke slowly, feigning a mixture of surprise and disappointment.

'That's not what I was expecting, Michele. You've let me down. My client is going to be very unhappy with this news. Do you think there's any way back? If you pay a little more, do you think your friends might miraculously find the missiles after all?'

'They say it's not about price. They say that the consignment is simply no longer available. And

I have my suspicions. I think I know who has screwed this up for us.'

Lucinda and James looked at each other and waited. Had news of Mitterrand's *volte face* leaked? Rigone continued, in a voice which was becoming more agitated.

'I think you have your suspicions too, James. I think you know who has fucked this up for all of us!'

James maintained an even tone.

'I'm still processing the news, Michele.'

'Well, I'm sure that you're thinking the same as me. It's Salvini. That cheap second-rate bastard. This has his name all over it. I don't know how he's managed to get in the way of our deal, but I know that he was fishing around in the market. I'm convinced that he has ruined this for me. And I will not let that pass! He has cost me. He has to know that I am not pleased, and I will make sure that he does. He will regret this!'

James was about to respond when the line went dead. Rigone had clearly said all that he had to say. He thought for a moment.

'How does that leave us, Lucinda? I guess I have to call Cortes and stall him somehow. I can string him along for another week or so, but then it's going to get difficult to convince him that this deal is still alive.'

'It's interesting that Rigone blames Salvini. I wouldn't want to be in his shoes now. Rigone sounds out of control.'

'On the other hand, if he threatens Salvini with reprisals, Salvini might begin to think twice about sourcing weapons for Cortes. Perhaps this will be good for us?'

Lucinda shrugged, and rose to go.

'I'll let Godfrey know what happened. But first we ought to double check the serial numbers against the ones Rigone gave us. Just to make doubly sure that consignment really is out of circulation.'

James was already at the door.

'We can get one of the Embassy cars to take us across town. We'll be there in twenty minutes.'

The lift in James's apartment block was tiny - barely able to accommodate two people. He and Lucinda squeezed in and drew the metal door behind them.

'You still wear Opium. I remember that from our time together in London.'

Lucinda smiled as she recalled their first meetings.

'We had a good time, Jamie. Actually, I think about those times. I mean, from time to time. Maybe after this assignment is over we can see each other socially from time to time?'

'Or maybe, a lot of the time? Do you have to rush off after we check the numbers?'

'Not really. I can hang around for a bit. Perhaps

we could have a drink or a bite to eat?'

'Sounds very good indeed.' The lift bell sounded, and James pulled back the door. 'Here we are. This won't take long and then we can have some dinner. Perhaps a return visit to Le Train Bleu?'

'Sure. I'd like that. Good idea!' Lucinda leaned against the doorframe as James found his keys and they entered the flat.

'The bedroom's through here. I keep all my classified things in a safe in there. Rigone's papers are with the....'

James had thrown open the bedroom door, and now stood motionless with surprise.

'Polly! But I thought that you were going to be out for ages. You said....'

Polly was bent over the writing desk, clutching a sheaf of papers. She reddened and pushed a hand nervously through her thick black hair.

'Oh Hi, James. I didn't expect....' She slowly regained composure. '....A change of plan. I had to....come back here for some essay notes, and I was....'

'But those are my things, Polly. Are they from my private papers?'

Just then, Lucinda entered the room behind James, and when Polly saw her, her look turned from embarrassment to fear. She started backwards, dropping the handful of documents on the bed between them. They all looked down at the file on top, with its Aerospatiale logo and list of serial numbers. James felt a sick panic rising in his chest.

'What's going on, Polly? What do you want with my things? How could these papers possibly be of any interest to you? Did you mistake them for some university notes?'

But Polly had her gaze fixed firmly on Lucinda. An awkward silence filled the room which it seemed no-one wanted to break. There were just too many lies to explain away.

Eventually, Lucinda spoke.

'I think we've reached the end of the road, Paolina. What do you think?'

James turned to Lucinda in confusion.

'You know Polly? What's going on? Have you and Godfrey been watching us?'

Lucinda walked over to the roof terrace, laid her handbag down and helped herself to a large Scotch from the drinks trolley.

'I said some weeks ago, James, that we make it our business to know everything about our officers, and who is watching them. You think you know Polly - what's the name you use - Peters? We know her by her real name - Paolina Petrenko. First year agent within the KGB's London station, recruited at the highest level by Mr. Komarov himself, and set to work to try to find out what you've been doing here in Paris.'

James sat back heavily onto the armchair in the corner of the room.

'Is this true, Polly? I thought that you and I had something really good together. Is it true that you've been using me like she says? I can't believe this!'

Polly had been silent as Lucinda spoke, and now she seemed resigned and her tone was flat.

'There's no point in me pretending, James. She's right. I'm sorry. The thing is, that I did grow to like you. It was difficult. Confusing.'

Lucinda clapped her hands together very slowly.

'How touching, Paolina. My heart bleeds.'

Polly turned on Lucinda, her eyes wild and her finger pointing in accusation.

'You bitch! You're not so squeaky-clean yourself! You've known all along about me, and you played along with it. You deceived James just as much as I fucking well did!'

Lucinda slowly drained her glass.

'But you forget, my friend, that he and I are on the same side. What I did was in his interests. He will learn to understand that. And by the way, as a matter of record, how did you work out his relationship with Hassan?'

Polly had calmed a little, and again seemed defeated.

'James is good, but he can be untidy. Important addresses scribbled on shirt cuffs. They were easy to follow up. I was there when he met the PLO guy. I heard enough to give Komarov the idea to set the rogue cell on to James and Hassan. And it almost worked.'

James held his head in his hands. This was too much.

'And the Falklands connection?' Lucinda continued. 'How did you know that James had been assigned a new role? That he had been drawn into the war operations?'

'Well, he came back from the Embassy one day, just as the invasion had begun. He had to fly to London suddenly. He showed me his air ticket, and it had been issued by HM Government. I reckoned he must have been called to London to be briefed.'

'And that's why we threw you off the scent with false locations, to try to confuse you and Komarov. He wasn't in Cairo, for example. That was all a fiction.'

Polly turned to James.

'I'm so sorry, Jamie. You were always very good to me. But this is who I am. It's just the way it is. And remember that for every lie I told you, you told me twice as many. You aren't the only victim here. We all are.'

'As much as I'd like to stand here and listen to your little words of wisdom, Paolina,' Lucinda replied, 'I'm afraid we have more important things to do. This is the end of this little escapade for you. I suggest that you gather your things and go. You're now at the mercy of Komarov and his people, so it's up to him whether he feels you have any further use, or if you're a walking liability.'

Polly suddenly looked crushed and exhausted, but then she was seized by a sense of urgency and anxiety. She grabbed a rucksack which was lying next to the bed, and hurriedly packed a few things - some clothes, some notes and some cheap jewellery.

James walked over to the roof terrace while she packed, and slid open the door. The cool evening air made a welcome change after the tense atmosphere of the room. He heard the door of the flat close behind her, and looking down to the street, he watched her as she hailed a taxi, which turned south towards the airport. Lucinda joined him as the taxi disappeared amidst the traffic.

'You knew about her all along, Lucinda, but you never said a thing. She couldn't trust me. It turns out that I couldn't trust her! And the thing that makes me feel sick, is that I bloody well couldn't trust you either!'

'Come on, Jamie! Don't be be so self-pitying! You said yourself that she was just a bit of fun. That you weren't serious. You'll get over it. The important thing is that we've done a good job for the Service. That's what matters. You've got to see that. Look, just forget her, and think of the future. Think about us. Everything is out in the open now. No more secrets between us? That's got to be a good thing hasn't it? Look - what about that drink?'

James went back into the bedroom and handed the Aerospatiale papers to Lucinda.

'I think you should go. We both need to think about this. I need to get my head round the whole thing. I feel like a bloody fool; I don't know what to think or who to trust.'

Lucinda shrugged, took the documents, and placed them carefully in her handbag.

'I'm sorry that this turned into a mess, Jamie. But when you've done your thinking, I'd like us to see each other. I'm going back to London tomorrow. There's still a lot of work to be done. Salvini is our biggest worry now and I'm sure you'll be needed to work on his case. And you're not a fool. Godfrey knows that you risked your life for this project, and I know that he values that. Leave all of that with me.'

Lucinda turned and made her way out to the lift, leaving James alone, looking across the rooftops to le Sacré-Cœur, just as he had done on that first evening when Polly had exploded into his life.

CHAPTER ELEVEN.
THE PLAN

A week passed. James had walked through the streets of the 5th and 6th arrondissements, turning over in his mind every moment he and Polly had shared over the past few months. He tried to see now, what he had missed then. But his conclusion was always the same. He had been naive and careless. His vanity had made him drop his guard. He was flattered by Polly's interest in him, and now he felt embarrassed and angry. It was all very well Lucinda making the case for him - that he'd risked his life for the Service, but he had known absolutely nothing of the source of that risk, and that made him feel even more frustrated.

But Lucinda was also right to say that their work wasn't over, and he forced himself to look ahead. He was impatient to meet with Godfrey again, to see for himself how the chief would regard him in the light of the recent 'mess' as Lucinda had described it.

So he was relieved to receive a call from François instructing him to fly to London the following Sunday to join a select working party at Century House on the Monday, to be chaired by Godfrey and Lucinda. Apparently his inside knowledge of Cortes combined with his City contacts made his inclusion in the group invaluable.

And now he stood looking west from the seventh floor penthouse terrace of Steve's flat. The sun was setting over the Hampstead skyline, and to the south, the lights of Westminster were appearing like fireflies through the evening haze. Steve handed him a Gordons and tonic, and retreated to the kitchen where he was preparing steak Diane and salad. Steve had bought the flat after his most recent promotion, and he had been only too happy to put James up while he was in London. James had invented a hurriedly-arranged research project to explain his trip. The flat was impressive; designed by Lubetkin in the 1930's, the building stood at the highest point in London amidst the pubs and restaurants of Highgate, where he and Steve had first met on their arrival in the capital.

'Come on through, Jamie. This is about ready. Grab a wine glass and a bottle of the Barolo on your way.'

'Thanks again for all this. I must repay the favour the next time you're in Paris. I have a bit more room in the flat now.'

'Yes. Sorry it didn't work out with Polly. I thought she was a lot of fun. She had a lot of interesting things to say. I like her. What went wrong?'

'It turned out that when it came to the big things in life, we saw things very differently. So it seemed best to part now rather than drag things out.'

'You mean marriage and settling down, that kind of thing?'

'Exactly. Just couldn't see eye to eye on a lot of things. This meat is delicious by the way. I'd rather concentrate on this.'

'Of course. Didn't mean to pry. But you know they say that one door closes and another door opens. What about that civil servant that you were so keen on last year? Lucinda, I think her name was? I wonder what's become of her?'

'Well, as it happens, I did bump into her recently, but our conversation was a little strained.'

'Oh well. Now you're in London, it should be easier to see her if you want to rekindle the relationship. Here. Have another drop of this wine. It's spectacular. And after this we can slip down to the Wrestler's Arms for a Guinness for old time's sake.'

James sipped the rich wine, which brought back memories of his time in Umbria with Lucinda. He told himself that he should be feeling a cold detachment about her. But he had to admit that despite everything, he was impatient to see her again.

James stepped out of the secure lift which had

taken him to the top floor of Century House, but on this occasion there was to be no waiting in side rooms. Instead, he was ushered straight into Godfrey's office. Around a dozen officers were standing in small groups, sipping coffee and looking across towards Parliament. The Union Jack was flying from the top of the Victoria Tower, and they could see the movement of morning commuters scurrying through the gardens below.

James could see that Lucinda and Godfrey were huddled in conversation at the end of the room. They began moving towards the top of the conference table and the rest of the group began to take their seats. Lucinda was sitting at Godfrey's right hand.

James hesitated as Godfrey looked across the room in his general direction, but then he seemed to focus and wave James towards him. He was to sit next to the Chief, at the top of the table. James was aware of surreptitious glances from the assembled group as they tried to work out his role and position. Godfrey's manner was affable and approachable and he exchanged pleasantries with a number of the officers. He had the elusive skill of making instructions appear like friendly advice. Sometimes his humorous asides would contain serious comments and officers quickly began to concentrate on what he said rather than be distracted by his appearance, which could most kindly be summed up as "having seen better days".

He turned to address the meeting.

'Very nice indeed to see you all here so bright and early. I know that some of you have been burning the midnight oil as we toil through the current crisis, and it is much appreciated. Now. I have asked Lucinda to put together a short agenda, and in a moment we will crack on with that, but first, I'd like to say a couple of words of thanks.'

'Firstly, I'd like to acknowledge the excellent work that Walter has been doing at GCHQ. As well as the direct work on the Task Force's security, he has successfully infiltrated the black market in arms, and has identified a number of attempts to secure Excocet missiles by a range of dubious characters, all of which, I am delighted to say, have ended in failure.'

James looked along the table to where a pale and slightly built young man was clearly uncomfortable at being thrown into the limelight. This was someone who distinctly disliked being the centre of attention. Under his suit jacket, his cardigan had been buttoned wrongly, and was sticking up over his suit collar.

Godfrey seemed to sense his discomfort, and moved on.

'I would also like to introduce James Gunn to all of you. James has been at the sharp end of the operation to render Cortes's efforts unsuccessful. He is the agent who has been the subject of much speculation within the Service and so I thought that you should meet James in person. He has been stabbed, injured in a car ambush, and narrowly escaped being blown up. And Lucinda tells me that he has been active in another very subtle role, as a fox to draw the hounds of the KGB onto his tail. It's very good to see you, James. In fact, it's a minor miracle that you're here at all!'

The group turned to James, nodding their approval, amidst a chorus of muttered congratulations. James sat back and tried to maintain an 'all in a day's work' expression. Godfrey had evidently finished his introduction, as he leant back and began to prepare his pipe. The slightest of motions towards Lucinda was her cue to take over.

'Right. Let's get started on the agenda. Three items. Report from the front, the problem of Salvini, and then the tiresome issue of the media and their inflated egos.

'Starting with news from the Task Force, the gains of late May mean that the army is now poised to move on Port Stanley. The next few days will be spent in meticulous reconnaissance and logistical build-up, preceding a brigade-sized attack commencing around the 11th. Walter and his team will be heavily involved in the preparations and we must be absolutely sure that there's no information leak. Which we'll come back to when we touch on item three.

'So, now we come to the continuing Exocet

threat and Roberto Salvini. Thanks to James's work, we've had the Argentine's lead acquisition officer - Felipe Cortes - depending on our efforts to source the missiles. This has gone very well so far, and James thinks that he can keep stringing Cortes along for now. But we should be aware that Cortes is also in touch with Salvini.'

Godfrey leant forward, put his pipe on the desk and spoke.

'Thank you, Lucinda - good summary. So, let's think about Signor Salvini. We've been giving some thought as to how we make sure that he's not in any position to source missiles. We have two ideas. The first would involve undermining the solvency of Banco Dolcetto itself. We're quite sure that he would use the bank's own resources to fund any missile purchases for the Argentines, and our finance team advise that were Banco Dolcetto to come under financial pressure, that would severely hamper Salvini's abilities. We know that Dolcetto is heavily in debt, and rather usefully, its main loan, which is from the Midland Bank, matures in two weeks. I suggest that James gets in touch with his main City contact - Percival Beloe - to do a bit of digging around. Let's find out who's in charge of the Dolcetto account at the Midland and think about how we can, shall we say, "lean on them". We have at least three ex-officers placed in strategic roles throughout the bank, and were Dolcetto - for "reasons unexplained" - to encounter difficulty in renewing its credit, then Salvini would have to rethink how he would pay for any significant purchase of missiles. Even if he was hopeful that the Junta could repay him.'

There were nods of approval around the table, and some suggestions of how the different departments might be able to contribute to the plan. As Godfrey paused to relight his pipe, a smartly-dressed officer at the end of the table spoke up. He was confident and self-assured.

'That sounds like an effective plan, C. And what's the second idea? You said you had two ideas?'

Godfrey sat back and his gaze momentarily turned to the paintings of cityscapes along the length of the wall behind the table. He wasn't inclined to rush his answer.

'Indeed I did, Cartwright. But on reflection, my second idea is probably not something which the Service would naturally choose to pursue. I raise it in order to dismiss it. Because to "terminate with extreme prejudice", as our American cousins would say, is not really part of our playbook. And in any case, I understand from Lucinda that Salvini has enemies who might solve our problem for us. Those include some choice characters with connections to the Italian Mafia, and who, it would appear, are seething with fury about Salvini's activities. No. I think that extreme measures are best left to our uncivilised opponents and to the pages of novels.'

Godfrey seemed amused by his own words, but

Cartwright persisted.

'But, do you think that Salvini is only a problem in the Argentinian context, sir? Or will he remain a threat to our interests once we've regained the Falklands? Do we know if he has a track record of supplying arms to other unfriendly States? If he's prepared to support the Junta, then surely he'd be willing to support the next rogue regime that threatens us?'

Godfrey was silent as he turned the question over. To Godfrey, who had fought in France, and spent the last thirty years immersed in the gruelling passage of the Cold War, such discussions were grave and oppressive. Cartwright was straight out of the University. He had yet to experience the harsh realities of their work. But Cartwright was the future, to be helped and encouraged.

'We will stick to plan A. You pose some very good questions, Cartwright, and I see your argument, but let's just focus our efforts for now on our friends at Midland Bank. Anything else just "wouldn't be cricket", as they say!'

Then in what seemed like an aside, he turned to James and whispered, 'Although as a Scot, I expect the rules of cricket are somewhat foreign to you?'

He turned again to the room, still smiling, and called on Lucinda to get back to the agenda.

'There was a third item for discussion I believe, Lucinda.'

'That's right. The wearisome issue of our friends

in the media. The PM is furious about the recent Panorama analysis of the war, and ministers are calling some parts of the media, particularly the BBC, "odious and subversive".'

Godfrey looked pained, and began rearranging the papers in front of him in an uncharacteristically irritated manner.

'Do we really have to discuss this nonsense?' he asked impatiently. 'I understand the PM's frustration, and I find the pomposity and self-importance of some of our media friends quite ridiculous, but can't we just lean a bit harder on them? Who's our media contact here?' Godfrey looked around the table. 'Who's supposed to be handling this?'

'It's me, sir.' A hand raised somewhat reluctantly at the end of the table. Godfrey peered in its direction.

'Of course. It's you, Proby-Smythe. Look. Can I ask you to have a word with the powers that be at the Beeb, and get them to heed the PM's words?'

'Of course, sir. But to be honest, we're a bit caught in the middle. We're all for a democratic free press - that sets us apart from the other side. But we're also trying to win this war and protect that freedom. It can create conflicts and....'

Lucinda interrupted and turned to Godfrey.

'Sorry to cut in, but you should know that there's another more serious dimension to the media question, sir. Commander Woodfield has voiced some grave worries about the BBC's leaking of strategic information which may have helped the enemy to prepare its defences. The Beeb reported on the planned assault on Goose Green before the action took place. Woodfield is convinced that the report lost us the initiative, and may have had even more serious consequences.'

Godfrey groaned, and turned again to Proby-Smythe.

'I understand that they have to deal in facts and 'the truth' as they see it. But that's the problem. It's as they see it. I understand that their job isn't to maintain British morale, but sometimes they go too far the other way. They risk losing the support of the people who're paying their fees. What's the good of an organisation like the Beeb if its own audience is suspicious of its bias?'

Godfrey was keen to conclude the meeting, but at the same time, he wanted to be supportive of his young colleague, who was right to raise all the sides of the argument.

'On second thoughts, perhaps this is all a little bit more difficult than I thought. Why don't you pay a visit to the Home Secretary straight after this meeting. Tell him I sent you. Ask him to have a word with the Director General at the BBC. Get him to impress on him that he's free to report on the war as he wishes, but any more slip-ups and leaks over the next week, and there will be serious consequences for him and the Corporation. Any push back and he's to remind the DG that the Chief has some intriguing files here at Century House. And that those files remain private. *For now.*'

Proby-Smythe seemed cheered by this, and nodded his understanding.

Godfrey pushed his chair back and shook hands with those closest.

'Thank you, all. Let's get on with our day. Lots to do. Thank you. Thank you...'

Godfrey's voice tailed off as he walked slowly towards his desk, but then he turned back to the retreating group.

'Oh, I wonder if you could you stay behind for a moment?'

He seemed to be looking in the general direction of Lucinda and James, who both turned to face him.

'Just James, if you please. I will catch up with you later, Lucinda. Thanks for running the meeting.'

Lucinda raised an inquisitive eyebrow, and backing out of the room, left James and Godfrey to settle down to their conversation.

Lucinda was waiting outside Godfrey's office for James to reappear, and she walked with him to the lifts.

'What was that all about? Anything interesting that you can share?'

James was quick to answer. 'Just some technical details about Midland Bank's accounts. He wanted to make sure that I knew how to approach my boss in the City to get the ball rolling on his plan.'

'That all? You seemed to take your time in there.'

'No. Nothing else. Don't tell me that you're becoming paranoid about Godfrey? It's bad enough inhabiting this ministry of misinformation and duplicity without losing trust in yourself! You are very firmly his number one. That's clear for all to see.'

Lucinda relaxed, and when they reached the ground floor reception she drew him to one side and they sat down on one of the battered sofas, which were carefully chosen to give the public face of the organisation an air of dreary anonymity.

'The meeting went well. I told you that you didn't need to feel bad about the whole Paolina episode. I've spun the whole thing in your favour.'

'Yes. I noticed that. Thanks. Look. I've been thinking about her and what you said. You're right. I was never going to be serious about her. I like her a lot, but in the end I would've been stringing her along. And I've come to terms with what she was doing. I'd like to tell her that I've no grudge against her, and that I've moved on. And to wish her luck.'

Lucinda was enthusiastic. 'That's really good, Jamie. I'm pleased. I mean, it's for the best. We should be looking to the future. I don't blame Paolina one bit. She was doing her job. In fact, I feel a little worried for her safety. Komarov and his people are not known for their generosity towards agents whose cover has been blown. I think there could be a way of bringing her across to our side to provide her with some security, and then to decommission her. I'd be keen to put in a word on her behalf.'

'Thanks. If she gets in touch, I'll let her know that we want to talk to her.'

'And meanwhile, where are you staying in London? Did I tell you that I've bought a new place in Primrose Hill? A townhouse overlooking the park. It's probably a bit big for me on my own. I'm rattling around in it.'

'Sounds amazing. I love that part of town. I'm actually staying with Steve for now, but I guess I'll have to look for a permanent place at some point. I had a message from Beloe this morning. He and Godfrey both want me back in London full time.'

'You must come round to my new place for supper some time. Perhaps after next weekend? The lead up to this final push on Stanley will keep me busy round the clock till then.'

They walked together to the taxi rank next to the petrol station, and he opened the door of the first cab.

'See you very soon, Jamie.' Lucinda stepped into the taxi, her damaged briefcase clutched under her arm, and he watched the cab head off towards the river. He took the next cab and set off north towards Highgate. There was no doubt that Lucinda was Godfrey's number one. But were there some things that even the anointed successor shouldn't know? Sometimes ignorance was the greatest form of protection. He was deep in thought when the traffic slowed to a halt on Westminster Bridge. He looked across to where the bridges of London sat one behind the other, as the river bent east past Waterloo and all the way to Blackfriars. Then the traffic cleared, and they began to move off. James settled back into the leather seats, his thoughts now clear and focused.

CHAPTER TWELVE. VICTORY

James spent most of the week in meetings with Beloe at the Leclerc Proust offices in Moorgate. He did as Godfrey had instructed, and Beloe had known exactly who to approach at Midland to discuss the Banco Dolcetto account.

Beloe also explained his thoughts about James's return to London. When his 'sabbatical' was over, Beloe wanted him to head up a new research team which the firm was developing. He had done a fantastic job during his time in Paris, and now he was needed back at base.

At the weekend, James returned to Century House where the news from the Falklands was continuing to improve. On the evening of Sunday 13th June, he was discussing the Salvini case again with Godfrey and two special operations agents, when news came in of an assault on Mount Tumbledown by the Scots Guards. It had been successful, and with that last natural defence line broken, Stanley itself was in sight.

Godfrey reached across his desk to where a red phone was ringing. He held the receiver under his chin as he lit his pipe. He listened for a few moments, then saying nothing, carefully replaced the receiver.

'Any plans for tomorrow, James? I hope not, because you would be cancelling them. That was number 10. We're required in Downing Street tomorrow morning, and it may well be a long day. The PM wants a tight group of relevant parties to man an operations room at number 10 itself, such is the anxiety about misinformation and leaks. If the operational momentum continues on the islands, then by this time tomorrow, we may have a resolution. I'll also want Lucinda and Walter with us. I'll brief them now. I'll see you first thing tomorrow. Ask the secretaries desk outside to get you a pass for the PM's office.'

So the next morning, James found himself striding along Downing Street, past the news cameras which were already watching every movement in and out of the famous black door. It was opened as he approached and he was led across the black and white chequered floor of the hall and up the impressive staircase, as the eyes of prime ministers past looked down on him from the portraits lining the walls.

'This way please, sir,' the secretary urged. 'We're almost there. We've reorganised the Green drawing room as the PM wished. In fact she has just popped in. Have a good day, sir.'

The secretary pulled back the double doors

to reveal a hive of activity, with senior military officers grouped around trestle tables laden with communications equipment, maps, and files. In the centre of the group stood Godfrey and Lucinda, who were engaged in an animated discussion with the Prime Minister. Suddenly the room fell silent as she began to speak.

'I have asked you to assemble here today as I believe and pray that our mission may soon be over. I spent the day yesterday at the Naval headquarters at Northwood, and throughout the day, and again overnight, the reports were favourable. I will now meet with my Cabinet, and I hope for continued good news during the course of the day.'

Accompanied by Lucinda, she then turned and walked briskly towards the double doors where James was standing. As she passed him, she paused, briefly.

'Mr. Gunn. Very good to see you again. And in one piece, I see, against all the odds. Good work. Very good work indeed.'

'Thank you ma'am. Always pleased to help.'

Lucinda smiled and winked at him as she followed the Prime Minister, who was already striding past the portrait of Elizabeth I, heading for the Cabinet room.

James passed what turned out to be a rather dull and frustrating morning, filled with endless cups of coffee, and periodic squints through the gauze curtains at the ever-increasing forest of cameras which lined the other side of Downing Street. Around lunchtime, just as he began to feel utterly redundant, a great excitement arose amongst the ranks of military men manning the phones and teleprinters. It was clear that a breakthrough had been reached. Godfrey emerged from the crowd of uniforms, and approached him with some urgency.

'James, it looks like the Argentinian force around Stanley is weakening. We are enforcing a complete news blackout, so the crowd outside will have to wait for a while yet. What we really need is some indication of the mood in the senior ranks within the Junta. The Task Force commander wants you to contact Cortes and establish his disposition.'

James was relieved to have a role at last.

'That's easy. He always takes my calls right away. If the room can stay quiet for a moment, then I'll call him.'

And so, the entire drawing room fell silent as James dialled Cortes, and activated the speakerphone. After a few moments, Cortes's secretary answered.

'Bonjour. L'office du commerce Argentin. Comment puis-je vous aider ?'

'Je voudrais parler à M. Cortes, s'il vous plaît. C'est urgent. Dites-lui que c'est M. Gunn.'

The line fell silent. Godfrey lit his pipe, adding to the heavy shroud of cigarette smoke which filled the room. Someone opened a window, but then shut it again sharply as the noise from the waiting pack of journalists filtered into the drawing room. Suddenly Cortes answered. His voice was subdued.

'Cortes. Is that you James?'

'Yes, it's me Felipe. I thought I'd give you a quick call just to say that we're still hopeful of getting our hands on the missiles from our Italian contact. How are things with your people?'

'We're all frustrated. In fact, things are worse than bad. This source of yours is proving to be a big disappointment. I might as well let you know that I've been talking to another party.'

'Well, now you're disappointing me, Felipe. I guess you mean Salvini?'

'Look. We never had any kind of exclusive arrangement, James. My other source is a much bigger enterprise, and they gave me a lot of hope; even up until yesterday I thought that they were going to beat you to the deal. But the news this morning is bad. It would appear that they've encountered some serious financial difficulties. They tell me that any hope of their delivering even one Exocet seems to be vanishing fast. But what the hell - I fear that I've run out of time in any case.'

Godfrey gestured to James to keep him talking.

'In what way, Felipe? You sound a bit gloomy. Aren't things going your way?'

Cortes's voice was despondent. 'This has to stay strictly between us, James, but I'm hearing some worrying things from home. Galtieri is putting pressure on Menéndez, our governor in the Malvinas. Galtieri insists that there should be no surrender until half of our combat groups have been wiped out. I think he's gone crazy, and now Menéndez is cracking under the pressure. He's going to disobey him.'

A suppressed excitement was now filling the room, and Godfrey motioned the crowd to remain silent.

'But that sounds like it's the end! Are you sure about your facts?'

'It's a shambles. I think we're finished, and as for me - well put it this way - I'm activating my exit plan. It's going to be too hot for me back in Buenos Aires once the islands have fallen, so I will be staying in my little hideaway in Madagascar for the indefinite future. In fact, I have to run. It's a shame that we didn't manage to do business. Perhaps another time, James.'

The phone line went dead, and the room was filled with exuberant voices. Godfrey remained impassive.

'Good work. That confirms what we're hearing. I'm going to the Cabinet room now to start making plans for this evening. It's only a matter of time before there's a formal surrender. I'm going to suggest that the PM aims to speak to the Commons around ten o'clock. That way ITN news will get the story, which will appease those obsessives who are more interested in winding up the BBC than anything genuinely important. It's all so tedious! I'll see you later. Must dash.'

Members of the naval team descended on James with congratulations and questions about his role, and the afternoon and evening passed quickly, as news from the front continued to spell the end of the conflict. Sandwiches were brought in on trays, and then a drinks trolley appeared, laden with bottles of beer and wine. Lucinda and Godfrey reappeared in the evening to say that they were being driven to the Commons, and that the PM was planning a statement to the House around ten fifteen.

A television was wheeled into the drawing room, and James and the others crowded round as the news lit up the screen. When the Prime Minister told the House that "they are reported to be flying white flags over Port Stanley", a great cheer went up, and one of the Army chiefs opened a bottle of Pol Roger with a great flourish. The sounds of cheering began to rise up from the crowds outside, and James found himself swept along, champagne glass in hand, down to the terrace and into the garden, where the staff and secretaries were celebrating the news.

It was almost midnight when Godfrey and Lucinda returned. Godfrey looked no less anxious, despite the news. He was already focusing on the terms of the Argentine surrender, and he was ushered straight into another meeting. Lucinda, on the other hand, looked radiant and exhilarated. She walked purposefully across to James, and kissed him briefly on the cheek.

'Good news at last, Jamie! You should have seen the reaction in the Commons! Everyone waving their order papers. Foot and Steele urging the country to rejoice. And now there's a crowd outside singing 'Rule Britannia'!'

Lucinda noticed that they were attracting sideways glances from the Downing Street staff, so she composed herself and taking his hand they returned to the building.

'The PM'll be back any minute. Come out to Downing Street with me and we can be part of the welcome party.'

Before he could resist, she had led him outside and into the group of Special Branch men waiting for the PM's car to push through the crowd. One of them double-checked James's ID as he had noticed the faint outline of the Walther PPK which was nestled inside his suit jacket.

The noise of the crowd rose, as the PM was stepping out of her car and beckoning to Lucinda to walk with her towards the waiting reporters. Lucinda and the security detail stood a foot or so behind her, scanning the crowd and the photographers. The PM was in ebullient mood. She gave the journalists the quote which they would print in every morning edition:

"We knew what we had to do, and we went about

it and did it. Great Britain is great again!"

James thought that he should feel more excited by the day's events. But he didn't feel like rejoicing. Instead, he felt relief that the bloodshed would stop now, and a quiet satisfaction that he had played a small part in the outcome. His credentials as a trader in arms were still unproven, and he wondered if there had ever been any genuine sellers of the Exocet on the black market. He would never know. But if there were, the enemy had failed to find them, and that was the most important thing.

Lucinda and the Prime Minister were beginning to move away from the journalists who were calling for more photographs and soundbites. James turned back to the black door, which opened to let him through. The communications team was gathering in the hallway to begin a long night of briefings for the US press and Fleet Street.

He felt that he had played his part, and was no longer needed. It crossed his mind that Steve may be working late next door at the Treasury. He would call the flat in Highgate and if there was no answer he would ask one of the No. 10 secretaries to try to track him down. He had an appealing vision of the two of them sinking a few late pints across the road at The Red Lion in Parliament Street.

But Steve was back in Highgate. He picked up the phone after a couple of rings.

'Jamie! Where are you? Have you seen the news? It's a bloody relief that it's over!'

'I happened to be kicking around Whitehall and thought you might still be down here, but no matter, I'll take the tube north and we can celebrate at High Point.'

'Sounds good! In fact, I'm glad you called. Polly was on the phone a little earlier. She sounded a bit strange. I don't know how she got my number, but she asked if you could call her when you have a chance. She sounded quite anxious, Jamie. Do you think she's OK?'

'I haven't spoken to her for a while, to be honest. I'll give her a call now. Give me her number and I'll find out what she wants. It's late, but I guess there's a chance she'll want to meet, so don't wait up for me.'

He recalled his conversation with Lucinda, and that he'd said he no longer felt any bitterness towards Polly. But now that he was dialling her number, he was less sure. The phone rang for almost a minute before she picked up. Her voice was barely audible.

'Hello. Who is this?'

'It's Jamie. Steve gave me your number. He said that you sounded worried.'

Her voice became clearer, and she sounded relieved.

'I'm so glad you called, Jamie. I didn't know if you'd want to talk to me after what happened in Paris.'

He suddenly felt a rush of warmth and fondness

for her.

'Let's put that behind us, Polly. Neither of us can exactly claim the moral high ground. Are you OK? You sound like you're in trouble.'

'Thanks. I really appreciate that. And you're right. I'm not in a good place. I had my debriefing with Komarov and his people at the Trade Delegation building. It's actually not far from where you're staying. Anyway - he didn't seem to be very interested in what I had to say. Of course, he already knew about the Armed Revolutionary Faction cell who've been targeting you, and I didn't have much information about your work on the Falklands, apart from those missile serial numbers which I had noted before I left. I never knew what the Russian official stance on the Falkland conflict was. I wasn't told.'

'But that all sounds pretty straightforward. Why are you so concerned?'

'I feel as if they've cut me loose. I got the distinct impression that I've become an inconvenience....one that they'd be happy to get rid of. I'm staying in digs in Whitechapel, and I'm very much on my own. I think I'm being watched. I think I'm losing my mind! I keep thinking that I've seen someone who's tailing me. I'm scared, Jamie. I didn't know who else to turn to.'

Although James was sure that he was over her, he was still fond of her and he wanted to reassure her somehow.

'Let's meet and talk about this. I'm sure that there's a way of getting you into a secure place. In fact I had a brief discussion about that very recently. Let's meet somewhere quiet - maybe in the City. All the victory parties are here in the West End. The City will be deserted as usual. Can you get to Leadenhall Market? Say - in half an hour?'

He could hear the relief in her voice.

'Of course. Yes. I'll set off right now. I can't thank you enough.'

He put down the receiver and for a moment considered finding Lucinda amidst the crowd to bring her up to date, but he knew that she would still be with the PM, and there wasn't time to waste. He asked one of the office staff how he could exit onto Horseguards, and they led him through the garden, past the police guards and into the parade ground. The street lamps lit up the expanse of white gravel and picked out flag-waving groups drunkenly meandering towards The Mall. He ran towards Admiralty Arch and pushed through the gathering crowd flinging himself into a passing taxi. His mind raced as they sped along the Strand. He would take Polly back to stay at Steve's flat, and in the morning he would arrange for them to visit the MI6 offices in Carlton Gardens where her future could be assessed. He hoped that she would be regarded as a low-value asset, one which could be easily re-integrated into some sort of normal life.

The cab dropped James in Gracechurch Street, and he walked east to the centre of the market which was deserted, just as he had expected. Huge hexagonal lanterns hung from the spine of the roof throwing their light onto the ancient cobblestones below. The giant curved hooks, hung with meat and poultry during the day, cast long shadows over the ground. His footsteps echoed off the walls of the shuttered shops and restaurants, and the only other sound was his breathing, as he picked up pace and made his way to the market's centre. Here two thoroughfares met in a giant cross.

Silence, and emptiness. Had she had second thoughts? Had she been stopped as she made her way to meet him? Had her fears been real?

But then suddenly she appeared from the shadows of one of the shop doorways. She was wearing the fake fur coat that she used to wear in Paris, and she had drawn it tightly around herself as if it would protect her from the world. She pushed her hair out of her face, and smiled with relief.

James breathed easily again. She was OK. He would protect her, and make sure she was safe. Everything was going to work out fine.

He took a step forward, arms open and ready to embrace her.

When the shot came, it came from above, the sound resounding off the walls and the great arched roof. The bullet hit her on the shoulder, knocking her backwards. A spray of blood formed an intricate pattern on the window behind her, and she fell, still smiling, onto the ancient worn stones of the marketplace floor. James swung around, and, pulling his pistol from its holster fired two rounds towards the roof of the market. Another shot rang out striking Polly in the stomach, her body twisting with the impact. But this time he had seen that the shot had come from one of the round windows of a restaurant at the very top of the building. He fired another couple of shots and saw the silhouette of their assailant as he moved back into the shadows.

Glancing round he caught sight of a heavy butcher's trolley. He grabbed its handles and pulled it over Polly, shielding her from the assassin and crouching under it he heard further shots ricochet off its heavy ironwork. He removed his jacket and pressed it against Polly's wound. She was slipping into unconsciousness, and was losing a lot of blood. Their situation seemed hopeless.

But just then, attracted by the noise of the gunfire, two street cleaners appeared on Gracechurch Street. They stood open-mouthed and frozen to the spot. James shouted towards them.

'Over here! We're over here! There's a woman with gunshot wounds and we're being fired at. Call an ambulance. Get an ambulance here as quickly as you can!'

One of the men ran to the nearest phone box, his

boiler suit flapping around his legs as he sprinted towards it. The other man began to approach James and Polly.

'What the fuck's going on here, mate? You alright?'

James reckoned that the gunman hadn't anticipated this interruption. He wondered if the silence from above meant that their attacker was considering making a run for it.

'Don't come any closer, pal. There's a crazy guy in the restaurant up there. I'm going to try to stop him. When I run, you come under this thing and look after the girl. Her name's Polly. Keep pressure on the wound until the ambulance arrives.'

James moved quickly, before his new assistant had time to think about the danger. He darted towards the entrance to the restaurant, and looking back, he could see a blur of blue boiler suit as the cleaner rolled under the trolley and started to help Polly.

He pushed at the door of the restaurant, which opened easily. The attacker must have forced it open earlier and taken up position in the building. He must have been following Polly, and James's arrival had messed up his plan.

The stairway to the restaurant was dark and steep. There was no sound from above. But as James approached the second floor, the slightest creaking of a floorboard made him fire upwards through the floor of the restaurant, causing a flurry of plaster and dust to descend. It covered his bloodstained shirt and made his eyes smart. He dropped down as two shots passed over his head and thudded into the wall behind him. In the confusion of smoke and dust, he bounded up the remaining stairs, and flung himself behind the heavy oak bar of the restaurant, firing into the room as he tumbled to the floor.

The restaurant was in darkness. The yellow light from the marketplace shone in through the round window and onto the bottles which hung in rows above his head. He could hear breathing from behind the table in the centre of the room. He tried to gather his thoughts. His shirt clung to his back, his pulse pounded in his ears and his eyes stung. He had to focus. He began to order his thoughts, and the first question he asked was how many rounds had he fired? After this magazine was empty, he was going to be defenceless. From the middle of the room he could hear the sound of a gun being re-loaded. He had to assume that his attacker had come better-prepared than he had.

Just as he began to think it was hopeless, a sudden burst of automatic fire sprayed over him, knocking glasses from the bar and shattering the bottles on the optics. James covered his head as glass rained down. Was this a prelude to a head-on assault? He reached round the corner of the bar firing his last two shots in the direction of the attacker. A few pieces of glass tinkled to the ground, leaving them in silence. After a few moments,

James could again hear low breathing. He huddled further under the bar, pressing himself against the cleaning materials, boxes of candles and assorted cloths and brushes which were stored there. He was out of ammunition, and would only have one chance to rush his attacker. He looked in dismay at the smashed vodka and gin bottles. Oh, for a dry martini right now to sharpen his wits! How was he going to get out of this?

Then suddenly, he had an answer. A cocktail! He grabbed a bottle of floor cleaner, and with a sigh, pulled off his tie and pushed its end into the neck. Alongside the candles, he found some matches. And then, crouching down, he lit the end of his tie and watched as the flame slowly made its way to the neck of the bottle, then launched it over the bar and into the room.

Seconds later a blinding flash lit up the restaurant, and he leapt forward to find his assailant waving his arms in panic, flames spreading over his legs and body. The man screamed as he tried to beat out the flames, but focused as he saw James rush towards him. He grabbed his weapon and despite the pain, aimed it at his chest.

James picked up a chair as he ran, and just as the machine gun was raised, he smashed into the attacker with all his force. Bullets peppered the ceiling, and they both careered through the room, scattering chairs as they went. James's foot caught on a table leg, and he fell crashing to the floor. He looked up as the human fireball continued to stagger backwards, and time seemed to slow as the writhing body smashed through the great round window and disappeared from sight.

He picked himself up, carefully pulling some pieces of glass from his hand. He had a few cuts around his head and neck, but he was OK.

He stumbled over to the broken window. A breeze was beginning to fill the room, mingling with the acrid smoke from the scorched carpets and furniture. As he gathered his senses, he heard the siren of an ambulance below, and looking across the marketplace he could see a group of medics around Polly. His courageous passer-by was with them. But all their eyes were trained on the wall below him. He held the edge of the window and leaned out carefully. Twenty feet below, the body of his attacker hung impaled on one of the butchers hooks. His automatic weapon lay on the ground a further twenty feet below him. His clothes were still smouldering.

James pulled himself back into the dining room, and picked up his charred Hermès tie as he crossed the room.

'Must remember to put that on expenses,' he thought as he made his way to the staircase and the exit. Police sirens were approaching as he reached the ground. He could wait and explain everything to them. But he couldn't do any more for Polly right now. And it would take a lot of explaining. It would take time, and right now all he wanted to do was confront the people who'd done this to her. They could have let her melt back into ordinary life. She didn't pose a threat to them. Why had they tried to kill her? He would make his way to Highgate, and in the morning he would beat on the doors of the Trade Delegation until Komarov himself gave him the answers. Now police cars were turning into the marketplace, sirens blaring. James kept to the shadows and ran south towards Fenchurch Street. A crowd of officers and medics gathered behind him as he slipped, unseen, into the night.

CHAPTER THIRTEEN. REVELATIONS

The spire of St. Michael's rose up against a pink sky as daylight broke over Highgate. It was early, and West Hill was deserted. It had been the dead of night when he had let himself into Steve's flat, and cleaned up his cuts and bruises. Along with the scar from the beating he'd taken in Italy, they made him look like a veteran, if not very competent, bare-knuckle fighter. He eased a fresh shirt over his aching shoulders. It was going to be a warm day, and he pulled on a light linen suit, and searched for as serious a tie as he could find; his old college one would do nicely.

He was going to confront the Russian and make a plea for Polly's safety. He knew he was breaking all the protocols, but Komarov already knew who he was, and in any case, a more conventional approach through the normal diplomatic channels would just get stuck in a bureaucratic quagmire. Better to challenge him head on.

The Trade Delegation building was set in several well-protected acres between Highgate West Hill and Hampstead Heath. Rolls of razor wire sat along the high wall to the estate which ran down the steep winding road. At its heavy metal gates he stopped and pressed the discreet intercom set into the wall. It was answered immediately, and James knew that he was being watched from the security cameras set high on the perimeter wall.

'We're closed. Get an appointment and come back at a civilised time of day.'

He saw no point in wasting time in small talk.

'My name is James Gunn. I want to meet with Comrade Komarov. It's about one of your people - Paolina Petrenko.'

'I think that will be impossible. We don't have anyone here with that name.'

James persisted.

'Look. I know that he's based here. I know who he is and what he does. I work for the British Security Service. One of his agents was attacked last night and I would be very interested to know why Comrade Komarov decided to turn on one of his own loyal employees. If you don't mind.'

This time there was a long pause. A milk float slowly made its way up the hill, and for a moment he was distracted by this very ordinary image of daily life, before his thoughts were interrupted by the crackling of the intercom.

'Even if there was someone of that name here, do you think that he would just wander out of our gates and have a friendly chat? You're not being very realistic Mr. Gunn.'

'On the contrary. I would expect him to meet

me outside the small wooden gate at the west side of the estate which leads directly to the Heath. And I'd expect him to be accompanied by a couple of security guards who would check me over for weapons, and who'd then walk several paces behind us. Just as a bit of insurance, as it were. Is that realistic enough for you?'

Another long silence. The milkman gave him a cheery wave as he drove slowly past. After a couple of minutes, the voice was back.

'Walk round Merton Lane to the west entrance. Wait there.'

James did as he was asked, and waited next to the very unremarkable gate on Millfield Lane. Ivy clung to its frame, and its dull green paint was peeling in places. It was eventually opened by two very large security guards, their shaven heads glistening in the morning light. One frisked him, while the other walked ahead to survey the Heath, which was deserted apart from a couple of early morning dog walkers. He returned briefly to the entrance, and then re-emerged accompanied by a tall, well-built man dressed in a dark tailored suit, a blue Winchester shirt and a club tie. His polished brogues resounded crisply off the road as he crossed to offer James his hand.

'Mr. Gunn. Mikhail Komarov. I've heard a great deal about you. I'm pleased that we are finally meeting. May I ask, what happened to your face?'

James hadn't expected Komarov's appearance,

or the complete absence of any accent. Here was as handsome and refined an English gentleman as one could hope to meet.

'That's what I want to talk to you about. I've been caught up in some messy situations recently, and people have been hurt: my injuries are nothing compared to some others. I think you can shed some light on what's been going on.'

Komarov could see that James was surveying his perfectly groomed figure.

'Not what you were expecting? Did you think I'd be wearing a greatcoat and a fur hat? We're a bit more sophisticated than that. If I'm to move around your upper class society, then I have to look and sound the part. Where do you think that I find most of my willing recruits? It's in the universities that you attended. I see that you're wearing your St. Gabriel's tie. A fine Oxford college. One that I know well.'

James was finding Komarov worryingly disarming. He tried to adopt a firmer tone.

'I'm here to talk about Paolina. I was with her last night, and I want to understand what happened. I don't know how badly she's been hurt, but I want to ask you to let her go. To let her walk away from your organisation.'

Komarov smiled, and putting a hand on James's shoulder, led him towards the Heath.

'I'm more than happy to talk about her. I believe that Petrenko's injuries are bad but she's going to be

OK. Let's walk up to the top of Parliament Hill, and we can talk as we go.'

They set off along the side of the bathing pond, and towards the open spaces of the Heath, Komarov's bodyguards following them at a discreet distance. He looked ahead as he spoke.

'I'm happy to help you. None of it makes any difference to me. I received a report on what happened in Leadenhall, and I can definitely say that we were not responsible. But we know who was. You have to think back to your time in Paris with Paolina. I recruited her last year. Her family have long ties with the Party, and it was easy to persuade her to work for us. I like her, and it's a shame that she's of no use to us now. But for a while she was extremely helpful. She knew about your meetings with Hassan. When she told me of his difficulties with the Armed Revolutionary Faction, I saw an opportunity to make trouble. I'm sorry, but it's what we do.

'We identified their most volatile group. There were four of them. We armed them and we briefed them. But after Italy, there was only one of them left. The guy that you left hanging on a butcher's hook last night.'

James was puzzled. Of course, he remembered that one of his attackers had escaped from the hijack in Umbertide, but why would he want to target Polly? Komarov continued,

'Think about the meeting that you were

supposed to have with Hassan on the day of the car bomb in Rue Marbeuf. What you didn't know was that it was Polly, as you call her, who set up the meeting. You were both supposed to die that day. Hassan narrowly escaped with his life, but you didn't turn up! So why weren't you there?'

James paused, and looked back at the silhouette of Highgate on the horizon as he recalled the events of that day.

'Because she delayed me. She was ill. And then she recovered. So are you saying you think she spoiled the plan? That she was protecting me?'

'Precisely. We worked that out during her debrief. And we think that from that moment she was as much a target for the Revolutionary Faction's revenge as you and your colleagues were because of your links with Hassan.'

James turned to Komarov, whose expression gave no indication of his thoughts.

'So, you're saying that she set me up and saved my life, all in the space of a day? I can see why you don't have any further use for her.'

'Exactly, James. But we didn't put her in hospital. If I'm guilty of anything, it's of not providing her with more protection when she returned to London. But to be honest with you, she's not a priority.'

'OK. So if we can agree that she'll play no further part in either of our lives, that would work for you? We offer her safety outside of our Service and I don't see her again?'

'Why not? As I've said, we have more important things that concern us.'

They continued up the curving path towards the summit, where they sat on a bench and looked down over the city. The dome of St. Paul's stood out against the straight lines of the City's buildings and as they looked along the skyline to the Centrepoint Tower, and further to the House of Commons, Komarov smiled.

'The Mother of Parliaments. There she sits complacently congratulating herself on the wonders of her democracy, while the poverty in the streets around her becomes more sickening by the day. Your world is founded on inequality, privilege and the deception of the masses. You must wonder sometimes, James, why you risk being shot at and stabbed for a corrupt system which the forces of history will inevitably overthrow. And the change won't come from your hypocritical middle classes, with their social guilt and feeble obsession with declaring their virtue. It will come from people like you. People from the working class who are now in a position to bring the whole decadent edifice crumbling to the ground.'

James slipped off his jacket, and rolled up his sleeves. He sat back and loosened his tie.

'That's a very interesting thought, Mikhail, but you don't convince me. I think it was Churchill who said that democracy is the worst form of Government except for all the others that've been tried. You can hide behind your discredited ideology as much as you wish, but the reality of life under your Mr. Brezhnev is very different from the picture you'd like to paint. Your doctrine has brought nothing but suffering. Twenty million killed under Stalin. Maybe sixty million under Mao? Persecution and corruption. I don't think you're in any position to lecture me. And when Andropov takes over, he's going to inherit a disintegrating empire that he'll struggle to hold together. By the end of the decade, the Soviet Union will be finished.'

Komarov was laughing now, and the guards turned to look.

'Fighting talk, James. You've been listening to your Iron Lady. Well, you may be right about the future, nothing stays the same. But I would wager that your Prime Minister will also be gone by then. But for now, she attracts nothing but praise, and I have to say that her behaviour over the Falklands has surprised us a great deal. Our academics couldn't understand why two conservative capitalist nations should come to blows. Another hole in Marx's theories.'

'But you must have worked out that it was all just a diversion?'

'Of course. Our people on the ground could see that the whole thing was just a desperate attempt by the Junta to distract their people from their disastrous policies at home. As you'd expect, we ramped up our propaganda machine to say that this was a poor, third world nation, being suppressed by an ex-colonial State, pathetically trying to cling on to its imperial heritage. That kind of thing is guaranteed to divide your middle classes. They care more about their guilty past than confronting the challenges of today.'

James was intrigued by Komarov's candour.

'So what did you really think? It looked to me like the Soviets sat on the fence to see who would come out on top.'

'That's true. And we oppose both sides. But I have to say that we were surprised by the speed with which you assembled your forces. Not bad for a so-called decadent and economically weak country. Our generals were interested to see how a volunteer army like yours would compare in the field, to a conscripted one like ours. They didn't like the answer.'

James was keen to know if his efforts had made any difference to the Russians' thinking.

'What about the scramble to acquire missiles. What did you make of the way the war developed?'

A couple began to make their way up the hill towards them, stopping every few moments to throw a tennis ball to their dog, which was careering erratically around the path. Komarov smiled at the scene and then turned to James. His features were once again impassive and serious.

'That's the thing, James. I've just read a report by our rear admiral Popov. He talks about the technology that you and the Western Allies have developed. He talks in particular about your communications. His conclusion is that the next conventional war will be won by the force with the most advanced electronics. And I'll let you into a secret, James: it isn't us. The Falklands war has been a sobering wake up call for us. I foresee that your negative media and liberal historians will say that the war was only significant because it helped a political party get re-elected. But we know the truth, don't we? This 'little' war will have a very big effect in strengthening deterrence.'

Their conversation was interrupted as the excitable dog ran, barking, to their feet and dropped its ball. It looked at Komarov with innocent, expectant eyes. His bodyguards began to move towards them, but Komarov waved them back and threw the ball down the hill towards Hampstead. He pulled a neatly-folded handkerchief from his breast pocket and wiped his hands.

'You British never fail to make me laugh. You care more about your dogs than your people. We really should be doing better against you.'

He carefully re-folded the handkerchief and slipped it back into his pocket, then rising, he checked his watch.

'I must start my official day now. I hope I've been helpful. Get your people to collect Petrenko from the hospital when the time's ready. She's your problem now.'

James rose and put on his jacket.

'Thanks for that. And thanks for the conversation. You are not at all what I expected.'

Komarov smiled, 'More civilised?'

'No. More pragmatic. I thought that you would be an ideologue. A rigid upholder of the dogma.'

'Not at all. You know I think we're probably much the same. Simple morals are fine for a simple world. Most of the time our's is impenetrable. It's labyrinthine. We have to find a way through it as best we can, and just keep moving in the general direction which we believe in.'

They shook hands, and Komarov's men began to move slowly back down the hill towards Highgate. His expression had changed. Now it was light-hearted, almost mischievous.

'Oh by the way, I didn't answer your question directly. The one about your pursuit of those missiles. Well, we've been watching your actions very closely, and I suspect that you'll have some loose ends to tidy up over the next few days. My sources tell me that Banco Dolcetto will be bankrupt by this time tomorrow. And their president has gone into hiding. We're impressed, James.'

Komarov started off downhill, but then he turned and called back.

'Good luck, James. But only when your interests

don't conflict with mine.' And with a cheerful wave, he continued downhill, sharing a joke with his men.

James walked slowly towards the overground station at Hampstead, turning over Komarov's words as he went. He would go to meet Godfrey, confess to his meeting with Komarov, and share all that he had learned. He would brief him about Polly but he wouldn't see her again so as to honour his agreement with the Russian. And at last he would be able to meet Lucinda. And that meeting couldn't come soon enough.

CHAPTER FOURTEEN. SECRETS

Lucinda settled into her usual seat by the window of the River Restaurant. The head waiter attended to her at once.

'A glass of your favourite Scotch, Miss Latham?

Lucinda smiled.

'Yes. Thank you, Philip. I think I'd like the twenty-five year old this evening. I'm in a good mood and I'm meeting a special friend.'

'Of course. Coming right up. It's a pleasure to see you again.'

Lucinda sat back and enjoyed the view west to Hungerford Bridge. Its reflection rippled in the water of the Thames. She could just make out the figures of late commuters as they hurried south over its walkway. To her left, Waterloo Bridge looked like some giant platform from which the buildings of the City reached up into the evening sky. She was in good spirits and looking forward to finally spending some time alone with James. Her father was visiting London tomorrow and he'd be staying here at the Savoy. Perhaps the time had come to introduce him to James. She would have a word at the American Bar later, and make sure that they reserved a table for them.

She was savouring the delicious Balvenie when James arrived. His cuts and bruises had begun to heal, but were still sufficient to attract alarmed looks from the other diners. She stood and they kissed briefly.

'Jamie! It's good to see you. God! - what happened to your face? All those cuts and scratches. Did that happen in Leadenhall?'

'Afraid so. It turned into quite a scrap!' He grinned.

'I heard all about it from Godfrey. I was shocked to hear about Polly. I'd no idea that she was in that kind of danger. I feel so bad about what happened. Godfrey tells me that we're going to look after her. Apparently she'll be in hospital for a while, but she's going to be fine.'

James had settled into the seat by her side, and reached for the cocktail list. He had brought a carrier bag which he pushed under the table. Lucinda looked him in the eyes and continued.

'How do you feel about her now, Jamie?'

James put the drinks list to one side.

'I'll always be fond of her. And now I know more about what happened in Paris, I'm grateful to her in a way.'

'How do you mean, grateful? She was spying on you!'

'Sure, but now I also understand that she took risks for me.'

'OK. And now? What happens next?'

'We're over. Very definitely finished. I've given her old boss an assurance that she's out of our lives.' James paused to call the waiter over. 'You know, she also made me think about how much we really understand other people - even those that we're close to. Who can we really trust?'

Lucinda reached across the table and took James's hand.

'What about me? You know that you can trust me.'

He leaned across and kissed her. And they were about to kiss again when they became aware of the head waiter hovering behind them.

'Terribly sorry to intrude on your evening, Miss Latham, but there's a young man in the foyer who insists on speaking to you. He says it's a matter of importance.'

'OK, fine. Tell him I'll be right with him.'

Lucinda rose and straightened her jacket. She flashed a smile at James.

'To be continued, Jamie. Don't go away!'

James ordered a dry Martini and he was swirling the olive around his glass when Lucinda returned. She was clearly surprised by her meeting.

'That was Cartwright from Century House. He had some unexpected news.'

James sat back and sipped his drink waiting for Lucinda to continue.

'You know that Banco Dolcetto went under this

week? And you know that Roberto Salvini went missing?'

James shrugged.

'Sure. I've had several meetings with Godfrey over the past few days. I think he mentioned it.'

She leaned closer, and continued in a hushed tone.

'Well. Salvini's body was found early this morning hanging from Blackfriars Bridge. He had thousands of dollars and some bricks stuffed in his pockets. Apparently we don't know who did it.'

James remained unmoved. He seemed distracted by the passers-by in the gardens below. She was puzzled by his reaction.

'Jamie! He's dead. Did you hear what I said? Aren't you interested in who's responsible? You don't seem particularly bothered by the news.'

'Of course I care. It's a mystery. I agree that it's strange.'

Lucinda leaned back in her chair and studied him.

'Are you holding something back from me? Do you know something about this?'

James laughed. 'Come on Lucinda. Be serious. You're the boss. You've said before that there's nothing about your officers that you don't know. What could I possibly know about this guy's grisly demise that you wouldn't already be fully briefed on?'

Lucinda looked more relaxed, and took another

sip of whisky.

'It's just that this doesn't sound like our way of doing things. I can't believe that we would have anything to do with it. I guess that clues will emerge when we begin to get more details.'

Then suddenly she sat forward excitedly. 'Of course! It's obvious! Cartwright mentioned that he was hanging from a piece of blue nylon rope. James - you know that can only mean one thing.'

'Our old friend Rigone! That makes perfect sense. He vowed to take his revenge on Salvini, and now he's left his calling card. He must be behind this. So - mystery solved! Are you happy now? I can't believe that you thought I was holding something back. Remember what you said in Paris? No more secrets between us.'

He reached under the table, and pulled a narrow box from the carrier bag. It was beautifully wrapped and tied in a tartan bow. He handed it to her, and she excitedly undid the wrapping to find a beautiful crocodile skin briefcase, with Lucinda's initials and family crest engraved above the lock.

'I popped into Swaine yesterday and picked this up. Hope it lasts longer than the last one.'

Lucinda was delighted, and grabbing James by the collar, kissed him again.

'You said you'd get me a new one. I love it and I'm looking forward to showing it off to Daddy tomorrow. And I'd like to show you off as well!' She lifted her glass in a toast.

'Here's to no more secrets.'

James lifted his glass to hers, and smiled. 'I'd like to meet him very much. And I'm glad you like the briefcase. Now let's get down to business! Half a dozen oysters, and then the lobster! Let's call your waiter!'

It was almost midnight when they left the hotel. They walked arm in arm through Victoria Gardens and hailed a cab on the Embankment.

'Primrose Hill, please driver,' Lucinda said as they sat back, and she rested her head on his shoulder. They drove east, and then stopped at the traffic lights beneath the great edifice of Unilever house. He put his arm around her, and kissed the top of her head. Everything was going to work out just fine.

The cab moved off, and James looked back at the black river as it twisted its way towards the City. 'No more secrets' he murmured softly, as he studied the great arches of Blackfriars Bridge.

AFTERWORD

At the end of *The Soho Institute,* the central character had secured twin roles as a stockbroker for a London firm, and also as an MI6 officer. And he had been posted to work in his firm's offices in Paris at the end of 1981.

So I had two questions to address when I began to plan the sequel. Was there an interesting financial storyline playing out in France during early 1982, and was MI6 engaged in anything particularly unusual at the time? Fortunately for *Traders in Arms,* the answer was 'yes' to both questions. The French Government under President Mitterrand was finalising the terms of its extensive nationalisation programme, which provided the potential for dramatic stock price movements which in turn informed the first sub-plot of the novel.

Meanwhile, the outbreak of war with Argentina in April 1982 over the invasion of the Falkland Islands provided me with the main plot backdrop. Such was the level of anxiety about the possibility of

Argentina securing additional deadly Exocet missiles on the black market, that the UK Government funded MI6 to enable its officers to pose as arms dealers to compete with the enemy's efforts to buy the weapons. As Nigel West puts it in The Secret War for the Falklands; "..it was made clear that on this occasion money was no object.." He details one officer who was given a "free hand and a long pocket to do whatever was necessary to ensure that Argentina received no more Exocets".

The further one delves into that plot, the more questions arise, many of them with no good answers. Take for example, the role of Banco Ambrosiano and its subsidiary in providing funds for the acquisition of Exocets by Peru. What are the connections between those negotiations, Ambrosiano's reputed links with organised crime, and the fallout from the Argentinian defeat? Banco Ambrosiano collapsed in June 1982, and its Chairman, Roberto Calvi, was found dead days later, hanging under Blackfriars Bridge in London. The mystery surrounding his death has never been solved.

And finally, what were the wider implications of the British victory in the context of the Cold War? What did the Soviets make of a war that lasted 74 days and claimed 1000 lives? According to Russian military sources at the time, it would seem that the

Falklands War had a sobering effect on Russian military confidence far in excess of its scale and extent. According to Vojtech Mastny; "By widening the range of uncertainty about just how easy an attack on Nato might be - at the very time when the Polish crisis put the reliability of the Soviet Union's own allies in doubt - the Falklands drama thus further strengthened deterrence. By doing so exclusively by conventional means, the outcome also supplied arguments in favour of emphasising conventional rather than nuclear deterrence."

That, I think, is a fitting epitaph for all those who lost their lives in the conflict of 1982.

Further Reading:

Nationalisation, Compensation and Wealth Transfers : France 1981-1982, by Herwig M. Langohr and Claude Viallet, July 1985.
The Secret War for the Falklands. The SAS, MI6, and the war Whitehall nearly lost, by Nigel West, 1997
The Black Door, Spies, Secret Intelligence and British Prime Ministers, by Richard Aldrich and Rory Cormac, 2016
The Soviet Union and the Falklands War, Naval War College Review, by Vojtech Mastny, 1983

ACKNOWLEDGEMENT

With huge thanks to Beth for her tireless help and advice in editing Traders in Arms, and to David, Jamie and Nadia for the cover concept, design and execution.

ABOUT THE AUTHOR

Robbie J Robertson

Robbie studied at Edinburgh and Oxford before embarking on a career in The City. His first novel, The Soho Institute, is 5-star rated on Amazon, and introduced James Gunn, the broker/spy who features in Robertson's work.

Robbie lives and works in London and Umbria.

BOOKS BY THIS AUTHOR

The Soho Institute

James Gunn is a young man searching for a direction, a career to which he can commit.

He arrives in London from Oxford to start work at the mysterious Soho Institute.

Then a series of shocking events determine his future. And it is not the future he had planned.

Part spy thriller, part coming-of-age novel, The Soho Institute is set in London and Oxford in the Autumn of 1981 and is the prequel to Traders in Arms.

Printed in Great Britain
by Amazon